A Treasure to Die For

RICHARD HOUSTON

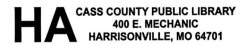

Version 2016.10.24

Cover Art by Victorine Lieske

ISBN-13: 978-998250014

DEDICATION

This book is dedicated to all my fans and loyal readers who have told me how much they love this series.

And to my family for all the time I spent shut up in my room to write this novel.

ACKNOWLEDGMENTS

The author could not have finished this book without the help of his editors and beta readers:

Elise Abram, www.eliseabram.com
Faith Blum, www.faithblum.com
George Burke
Bob Cherny
Lynne Fellows
Cheryl Houston
Robert Spearman

And for her great cover art, Victorine Lieske, www.bluevalleyauthorservices.com

CHAPTER ONE

For several months now, I've been thinking of ways to commit the perfect murder. It's not that I'm a violent man, or I'd own a Doberman instead of a Golden Retriever. No, it's because after I inadvertently solved a couple of murders, I thought I might try to write a murder mystery. Well, to be fair, Fred should get most of the credit for finding those killers, but I did help. He's great when it comes to fetching rocks and sticks, but really sucks at speaking, so together we make a pretty good team, like Scooby Doo and Shaggy.

Fortunately for Evanovich and Patterson, I couldn't get past the first chapter of my book. Good writers need to get into the heads of their characters and I couldn't for the life of me understand why someone would want to kill another human being. All that changed the day Shelia's boyfriend tried to kill Fred.

My brief journey into the dark side started like most days when I was between jobs, which lately, was far too often. Fred and I would spend half our morning walking around Evergreen Lake where a normal forty-five minute walk takes a couple hours if I let him swim and retrieve sticks. Little did I know then that I was about to get involved in a real murder.

Bonnie, my neighbor and friend, had talked me into joining her for a signing at a small bookstore in town. She had taken it upon herself to keep me busy ever since my wife, Julie, died last year. Bonnie thought I should be at the signing because the author was supposed to be talking about a hidden code in *Tom Sawyer*. She knew Julie had bought me a copy of the book on our first date. It was some kind of omen, she said, and insisted I had to go because a friend of hers, who bought and sold rare books, would be there and could tell me how much my copy is worth.

I told her I wouldn't sell the book for a million dollars and did everything I could to get out of going; including the fact that Fred would probably be soaking wet after his swim in the lake. That was when she insisted on walking the lake with us so she could help keep him out of the water. She would have better luck taking an alcoholic on a tour of Coors' brewery and not letting him sample the merchandise.

Luckily for Bonnie, Evergreen Lake isn't much more than a large pond with benches strategically placed where she could stop to catch her breath. Catching a breath for Bonnie consisted of lighting a cigarette and smoking half of it before flicking it into the water. She had recently turned sixty-nine, but refused to let her age stop her from living, as she put it.

About halfway through our walk, Bonnie needed another break and plunked her thin frame down on a nearby bench. "Let's take five, Jake. We don't want to be the first ones there." She was right, of course. I had a habit of always being too early, like the last time I picked up my first wife from work and saw her on her boss's lap. Sometimes it pays to be late.

"Sure, Bon, Fred needs off this leash anyway." We were on the backside of the lake, away from the fishermen and most of the morning crowd so I let him loose. He ran straight to a nearby stick and brought it back to me. I instinctively threw it into the water.

Bonnie tried to look perturbed, but her smile gave her away. "Jake, you promised he wouldn't get wet."

I answered with a frown when I saw her reach inside her purse for a pack of cigarettes. "And you promised to cut back on those."

Her smile faded to a pout while we watched Fred swim after the stick. I tried to forget I had agreed to sit through a boring reading by a local author. My mind had drifted to when Fred and I used to take these walks with Julie. Unlike my first wife who would yell and scream when Fred shook himself dry after a swim, Julie only laughed. Then she would shake her head so her ponytail would swing back and forth before picking up the stick to throw it back in the water. Julie had died just when I thought life couldn't get better.

Fred kept me from becoming totally depressed, and it wasn't long before I was back to writing how-to articles and doing odd jobs to pay the bills, even if it wasn't always on time. I knew the real reason I didn't want to go to the reading was because I was jealous. I couldn't for the life of me fathom how this guy was not only published, but made it to the *New York Times Best Sellers List* and was selling his book faster than they could be printed.

Bonnie woke me from my trance with a sharp jab of her elbow. "She has a nerve coming back here." At seventy-two-hundred feet, we were high enough to enjoy the warm morning sun and escape the haze from Denver, but not high enough to escape from its rudest residents. I didn't see Shelia and her boyfriend until it was too late.

"Hello, Bonnie," Shelia said, standing between us and the lake. She had been a neighbor of ours until last year when Bonnie tried to poison Shelia's husband.

Bonnie glared back and didn't say a word. Bonnie's daughter, Diane, had been killed in a terrible hit-and-run accident twenty years before. Then last year, I discovered the car that hit her was a Corvette owned by Shelia's husband. Only after the attempted poisoning did I find out the driver who killed Diane was Shelia.

Fred came out of the water, dropped his stick at my feet and started shaking like an unbalanced washing machine on the spin cycle. He started with a roll of his head and then really got into it with water flying off his neck and torso until every hair on his body was spraying Shelia and her friend like an untethered garden hose.

"Get that frigging mutt away from me!" Her friend yelled, before picking up the stick and raising it to hit Fred.

That was when I realized why people murder one another. I literally wanted to kill this jerk before he had a chance to kill my dog. I wasn't close enough to block the blow and found myself looking for another stick, or rock, to throw at the jerk who was about to kill my best friend. But then Fred's retriever instincts saved his life, or at the very least, a bruised rib. He was in the water and swimming toward where he thought the stick would land before the guy could hit him with it. Jerk lost his balance and fell into the lake when his downward thrust failed to connect with Fred.

Shelia screamed while I broke out laughing. It was better than the perfect murder. Even if he couldn't drown in the shallow water at this end of the lake, I still had my revenge without the threat of life in prison. The water temperature was barely above freezing, ideal for a Golden Retriever, but hypothermic for us less hairy mammals.

My laughter was cut too short when Bonnie broke her silence, pointing her cigarette at Shelia's face. "What are you doing here? I told you before I'd see you in hell if you ever show your ugly face up here!"

Shelia didn't back away, nor did she bother to help her friend climb out of the chilly water. "It was an accident, Bonnie. I told you before, I'm sorry. Why can't you let it go?"

Bonnie's eyes filled with tears. "She was only sixteen. She had her whole life in front of her."

I was captivated by a vision of a burning poker piercing Shelia's eyeball until a gathering audience woke me from my trance. A couple of joggers had stopped to watch the commotion, so I thought it would be best to put Fred back on his leash. Not because of the joggers, but because he might get it in his mind to help the person who had tried to kill him.

Jerk finally made it to dry land, shivering from his ice-cold bath, and walked over to us with a raised fist. "That mutt is dead meat! I'll get him and you for this!"

Shelia grabbed his shaking hand and pulled him away before I could answer. I was still thinking of a comeback when Bonnie beat me to it. "You harm one hair on his head, and I'll see you both in hell!"

Shelia didn't wait for her friend to answer, and dragged him away without another word. Bonnie turned her attention to the joggers and apparently surprised them enough with her knowledge of anatomical places to put one's finger that they decided to leave, too. Sailors and construction workers could learn a lot from her when she was upset.

Bonnie was still upset when we made it to the bookstore, so I kept on driving and parked outside the Little Bear bar a few blocks down the street.

"Why are you parking here?" She had been too busy fiddling with her purse to notice until I shut off the engine.

"Those things never get started on time, and even if it does, we won't miss much. How about we go sit on the patio where you can calm down with a cigarette and a drink?"

Bright sunlight shined through the windshield exposing every wrinkle in her tired face. She looked up at me with bloodshot eyes, holding the pack of cigarettes she had been looking for. "Thank you, Jake. That's a splendid idea. And then I can refresh my makeup in the little girl's room before we walk over to the bookstore."

By the time Bonnie recovered and redid her makeup, she was gabbing away about how she could spend the money if we could decode the location of the treasure the author wrote about. It wasn't until we entered the bookstore that her excitement ceased and she went quiet. The place was packed tighter than a revival tent in Mississippi. Using powers of deduction that would make Hercule Poirot envious, I quickly reasoned that the guy reading at the front of the audience with a poster next to his table that read, *Twain's Enigma by Paul Wilson*, was the author. He didn't bother to look up when we took a seat toward the back with my wet dog.

I already knew, without using any gray cells, that the book was about the somewhere near Breckinridge. Bonnie had told me all that beforehand, and the press had played it up because a similar book that sold a million copies recently made national headlines. Paul Wilson looked like a copycat to me.

The bookstore was small compared to the big-name stores in shopping malls scattered in and around Denver, but that was thirty miles and twenty-five hundred feet down the hill from our little town of Evergreen. I thought the place was quite cozy, even if it was cramped. There was only one chair left, so I let Bonnie have it and stood behind her, holding Fred on a short leash. He had dried off sufficiently, but not enough to ease the odor of wet dog. I suppose I was used to it, and didn't notice until a couple next to Bonnie got up and left. Fred looked up at me and smiled when I took a seat. I bent down to pat him on the head to let him know how lucky I was to have him when I felt an elbow in my ribs.

"It's him, Jake," Bonnie said, before poking me again. "It's that creep from the lake. And look who's sitting next to him."

I stopped massaging my side in time to see Shelia turn around and stare at us. Maybe she didn't know it was a pet-friendly bookstore, and Fred was a regular, or maybe she was simply surprised that Fred would be interested in literature. I expected her friend, the guy I only knew as Jerk, to turn around too, but he seemed far too mesmerized by what the author was saying. "Shh, Bon," I whispered, holding a finger to my lips.

Shelia snickered, then turned back to listen, too.

"But that's impossible," Bonnie whispered. "He was soaking wet only an hour ago. How'd he dry out so soon?"

Several people from the row in front of us turned and gave the universal sign for her to be quiet. It seemed to work and everyone went back to listening to the author.

"'Andrew Jackson Drakulich, or Drake as his niece, Penny, called him, removed the last pack from his frozen mule and stumbled to retrace his steps back toward the shelter of the abandoned mine. It was less than twenty yards, yet he could no longer see the path he had made just a few minutes earlier. Sixty mile an hour winds hid every trace of his return with several feet of new snow. Drake swore at the cold wind biting his face and continued toward where he thought the mine should be.

"'Once back inside, Drake struggled to close the splintered aspen door against the gale-force wind, and cursed again when the wind violently caught the door and tore it out of his hands like a kite from a child. Then just as viciously as it had been torn from his grip, the door slammed back as though connected to a coiled spring, and hit Drake full force on his outstretched fingers.

"'Drake had seen men's fingers crushed by misdirected sledge hammers before, a common occurrence among novice miners, and he could have accepted that, but nothing in his sixty-two years had prepared him for what the equivalent of a twenty-pound sledge could do in subfreezing weather. In that brief moment between realization and pain, he stared at his fingerless glove with all the astonishment of a gold strike. Then, before the pain completely hit him, and before the wind could blow the door open again, he dropped the latch beam in place with his good hand and screamed every obscenity he knew.'"

Wilson stopped to catch a breath and take a sip of water. It was just long enough for Jerk to cut in. "Can you get to the part of the treasure? The paper said you were going to show how Mark Twain put a secret code in his book on where to find a fortune in lost gold. It didn't say anything about you reading to us like a bunch of preschoolers."

The look on the author's face would have made Medusa jealous, but I doubt anyone noticed. Jerk must have changed his shirt, but his pants were still wet, making it look like he had a bladder accident.

"Craig, please. Not here," Shelia said, turning to face him. Her cheek was bright red, and obviously it wasn't because she had too much sun at the lake, or embarrassed by his remarks. Even I knew it would soon turn a dark blue. She should have let him drown.

I whispered a little too loud to Bonnie, "I think the name Jerk suits him better."

My remark resulted in a laugh from a few people next to us.

"I'm sorry if the news article was misleading, sir," Wilson continued, unaware of my joke. "My publisher hired a new publicist straight out of school who is trying to make a name for herself. The treasure in my book is folklore as is its location. I suggest if you are looking for a treasure hunt, then maybe you should go out and buy Forrest Fenn's book."

"Who the hell is that?" asked a kid sitting next to the jerk I now knew as Craig. He had the weirdest hair I'd ever seen. His head was shaved bald on one side and long, purple hair on the other.

"That guy who claims to have buried a treasure so people will buy his book, Cory. Now shut up and let him finish. Or have you forgotten why we're here?" It was the punk's girlfriend, or at least that's the impression I got. It could have been his sister, for all I knew. Either way, they were definitely a matched set with nearly identical tattoos covering their necks and arms.

"Thank you, miss," Wilson said. He began to read where he had left off, then looked back at the audience. "Well, considering how my publisher may have brought most of you here on false pretenses, I guess it won't hurt to skip ahead to the treasure. But please remember, this is historical fiction. I have simply taken an incident from the past and used it to create a story."

Wilson lowered his eyes again and started flipping pages. Fringed with graying hair, his shiny bald spot reminded me of my grandmother's doilies. He seemed to find the page he wanted, and woke me from my daydream of Grandma setting the table at Thanksgiving dinner. But instead of reading, he held a finger on the page, removed the glasses he kept on a rope around his neck, and raised his head. "I need to at least fill you in on some details first. The story is about an old miner, I call Drake, who in the late summer of 1895 went searching for the Lost Tenderfoot Mine in the hills above Breckenridge. Drake and his brother had lost their jobs working the silver mines of Leadville after the big crash of eighty-three. His brother needed money desperately so he could move his family back to Denver, where they could find care for his daughter, Penny, who was dying of consumption. The story of the lost mine had been around for nearly twenty years by then, and Drake had nothing to lose, so he went looking for it. Legend has it that some unknown Tenderfoot had brought out twenty pounds of gold in 1880, and couldn't find his way back. Miners and fortune hunters have been searching for it ever since.

"Anyway, Drake must have found the mine and dug out five thousand dollars' worth of nearly pure gold, for he left a message describing his find and the location of where to find his gold and the lost mine. However, according to an article I found in the *Rocky Mountain News*, his message wasn't found until some uranium miners stumbled on the remains of his pack mule in the early fifties. There was a frenzy of sorts, searching for the gold, but because Drake had encrypted the location in code, the treasure was never found, and it soon became just another forgotten fable."

"You're telling us there's only five thousand dollars?" It was Cory again. "I don't call that no treasure."

Wilson didn't seem to be very upset at the latest interruption. He smiled and looked back with cold, gray eyes at the kid. I'd seen that same smile before. I think it was Hannibal Lecter in the movie, *Silence of the Lambs*. "Well, son, that would be about twenty pounds at the price of gold back then. Do the math if you want to know how much twenty pounds of gold is worth today. Twelve troy-ounces per pound, times twenty, times twelve hundred dollars is a nice day's work. But of course, the real treasure is the mine itself. Crack Drake's code and you have wealth beyond imagination."

Cory didn't say another word. I couldn't see his face from where I sat, but I could imagine him counting on his fingers trying to calculate the sum.

Wilson didn't wait for the kid to come up with a figure. "That's nearly three hundred thousand, Son," he said before refocusing on his book.

He waited a moment for it to sink in then continued. "I think I left off where Drake had found shelter in an abandoned silver mine and lost his frostbitten fingers when the wind blew the mine door shut on his outstretched hand. I'll skip ahead now to the good part where he has started a makeshift fire from all but one book in his pack.

"'Drake huddled over the flames, trying to catch every last ray of its nefarious warmth, as the fire burned with the words of dead writers. Drake needed all the help Penny's friends could give him if he were to make the twenty-mile trek into Leadville once the fire died out. As he fed more pages to the fire, and watched them slowly die, he remembered a story Penny had read to him about how British spies would send coded messages keyed to a popular book. It was a simple code: a series of numbers representing a page and word count for each word of the message. The cipher would search the book for a word he wanted to use and then count how many words came before the chosen word on the page. To decipher the code, the spy simply found a copy of the key book, and wrote down the word corresponding to each pair of numbers.

"'Hours later, Drake finished his Last Will and Testament in which he says Penny's consumption will be cured when she solves his riddle. On the back side of the will, he put twelve lines of numbers, and a note telling her to read the story where a boy gets his friends to do his chores. Then he put Penny's copy of *Tom Sawyer* in his pack with the gold, and threw it down the shaft at the end of the mine.'"

"So you're telling us we got to buy your book to find where the gold is hidden?" It was Cory again. His tone suggested more than a question; it came out like an accusation.

Wilson answered condescendingly. "I told you, this is a fictionalized story of an article I read from a 1953 issue of the Rocky Mountain News. The book you want to buy, if you insist on believing the story is real, is written by Mark Twain, not me."

"And what book is that, Mr. Wilson?" asked a bald man in the front row, wearing worn Levi's and a sleeveless shirt that showed a crude tattoo of the Marine Corp symbol and the words, *Semper Fi*, beneath it.

Craig took it upon himself to answer for the author. "Jeez, dumbo, any idiot can see it's *Tom Sawyer*."

The bald guy in the front row turned to Craig, allowing me to see his face. There was real hate in his eyes, and for the brief second I saw him before he turned back, I thought he looked familiar.

"I'm right though, ain't I, Wilson?" Craig asked as though nothing had happened between him and the bald guy.

"Yes, but not just any copy of *Tom Sawyer*. You must remember, Drake wrote the code in 1895 and *Tom Sawyer* was first published in 1876, so it's anybody's guess which version was used. The wrong edition will throw off the word count."

Wilson was about to continue when a gray haired woman sitting in the row ahead of me raised her hand.

"Yes, Patty?" Evidently she wasn't his mother, or he wouldn't have used her first name.

"Perhaps the old miner was using one of the pirated Canadian versions." She spoke so softly, I had a hard time hearing her.

Craig was still standing and turned to face the timid woman. "A what version?" he demanded.

Wilson answered for her. "I believe the question was about Canadian versions that were copied from the London edition. Is that your question, Patty?"

She nodded her head without speaking.

Craig cut in again. "You mean my first edition might not be the right version?"

Wilson's eyes seemed to dilate. They had been a light gray, but were now pure black. "You have a first edition of *Tom Sawyer*?" he asked. "My God, do you have any idea what that's worth?"

Shelia, who hadn't uttered a word during the debate, suddenly nudged Craig in the leg and told him to shut up. "Look who's the idiot now. Why don't you tell everyone where we live while you're at it, so they can come and rob us tonight?"

"What? Who would steal that old thing? Didn't he just tell you we don't have the right copy anyway? And I don't need no woman telling me I'm a frigging idiot." He didn't wait for her to answer and stormed out without her, slamming the door so hard it shook the glass walls at the front of the store. Shelia followed on his heels. She reminded me of Fred when I yelled at him for doing something bad. I'm sure if she had a tail, it would be between her legs.

"Miss? Wait up. I need to talk to you." Those who were watching Shelia turned to see the old lady jump out of her chair and run after her; we had no problem hearing her this time.

Shelia looked annoyed, but slowed down long enough for the old lady to catch up. "Do I know you?"

They had everyone's attention, including the author. "I may have one of those pirate copies, if you're interested. Can we go somewhere and talk?"

Fred yelped when Bonnie jumped out of her seat and stepped on his foot. "I need to tell Patty your copy isn't for sale, Jake, before she sells it to them."

"You know her, too?" I asked, running after Bonnie with Fred at my heels. He wasn't limping, so I doubt if he was hurt, since she couldn't weigh a hundred pounds, and that's when she carried her ten-pound purse. She probably scared him more than anything. I caught her before she got to the door.

"Is that why you brought me here? To sell the copy of *Tom Sawyer* Julie gave me?" I asked before noticing we were now the center of attention. I turned to the audience and uttered a lame apology before leading Bonnie and Fred outside.

Shelia and Patty were in the midst of a heated conversation while standing next to a beat-up Camry not much newer than my Jeep. I could have been wrong about them arguing, but they were both waving their arms in the air like a couple of prize fighters. Craig had already started the car and was revving the engine. We couldn't hear the argument over his noisy muffler.

"Damn it," Bonnie said. Her posture spelled defeat. "I can't tell her now, not with Shelia there."

I felt bad for raising my voice, but didn't have time to say so before Shelia got in the car. We all watched as Craig raced out of the parking lot in a cloud of blue smoke.

Patty turned and came back toward us, smiling. She could easily pass for Bonnie's sister if I didn't know better. They each stood about five-two, had the same cloudy-blue eyes and didn't bother to dye their gray hair.

Bonnie bent down to Fred's level and held his head between her hands. "I'm sorry, Freddie. Did Aunt Bonnie hurt you?" Before he could bark his answer, she looked up at me. "I should have asked first. I thought you'd be happy to get the money for your book."

"Is this Fred the Wonder Dog?" Patty asked when she joined us.

Fred beamed and offered his paw.

"See, I told you, Patty. I swear he's human sometimes," Bonnie remarked.

Then turning to me, "Jake, I'd like you to meet an old friend. Patty, this is Jake."

Patty extended a frail hand. "I've heard so many wonderful things about you."

I didn't know how to answer. The first thing that came to mind was to say Bonnie must be smoking something other than cigarettes, but I held my tongue. Luckily, Bonnie broke the awkward silence before I put my foot in my mouth.

"I hope your friend doesn't think we were rude running out on his reading, but I had to tell you Jake's book isn't for sale."

Patty sighed before answering. "Why don't you tell Paul yourself when he drives me home, Bonnie? I'm sure he won't mind dropping you off first."

Bonnie looked confused. "Paul? Oh, the author."

Her blank expression turned ecstatic, looking at me like a teenager who was just invited to the prom. "Do you mind, Jake?"

I couldn't speak for Fred, but after the day I had, I didn't mind at all. We said our good-byes and headed for home.

I had completely forgotten about the incident at the lake until the next day when Fred and I made our way to Bonnie's for coffee before going on our walk, or in Fred's case, his swim. Bonnie lived just below us in a house built back in the seventies that resembled the structures covering old mines; she called it her mine shaft. Whatever architectural style one wanted to pin on it, it was huge compared to my little cabin and sometimes a little too close.

She put the television on mute after letting us in the back door. I helped myself to coffee while Fred went over to his bowl that Bonnie kept by her refrigerator.

"You came home late," I said as I took my usual chair at her kitchen table. I knew this because her television was off all night. I never watch much television, mainly because I don't own one, but Bonnie does. She has it blasting nearly twenty-four-seven, and I never miss an episode of *Doctor Oz* or *Ellen* when her windows are open.

She removed a spoon from her cup and looked up. Her eyes showed bewilderment. "What makes you say that, Jake?"

"Your TV wasn't on."

She frowned and went back to stirring her coffee. "Well, if you must know, that nice author took us to the Wildflower for coffee, then we all went next door to the Little Bear for a few drinks before he brought me home." Her tone suggested I was intruding.

"Sorry, Bon, just trying to make conversation," I said before jumping out of my chair to turn the sound back on the television when I saw the jerk from the lake flash by on the screen. The news reporter was saying something about a burglary and a murder. I grabbed for Bonnie's remote and hit the back button. She had a DVR that allowed her to reverse or pause whatever she had been watching.

Bonnie stopped stirring her coffee again. I once remarked that if she drank cream instead of coffee, she could turn it into butter. She pointed at the television with her spoon. "Isn't that's Shelia's new boyfriend? What's he doing on TV?"

"Shelia's been murdered," I answered, realizing Bonnie must have missed the part about Shelia checking out.

It looked like she was going to drop the spoon. Her face went blank, and she stared at the television before speaking again. "Murdered?"

"So it seems. Someone stuck her in the neck with a nail file and punctured her carotid artery."

The interview must have been live. The reporter, Paula Morgan, was shivering in the cold morning air while interviewing Mr. Jerk, AKA Craig Renfield. He, in turn, couldn't seem to focus on anything above her neck. "I came home from watching the CU game at a buddy's house and found the door wide open, and she was laying in the kitchen," he said without taking his eyes from Paula's cleavage.

Paula was too focused on the camera to notice where Craig was looking. "Was it a burglary gone bad?"

"How would I know?" He seemed annoyed, having his concentration interrupted. "I ain't no psychic."

Paula rolled her eyes for the camera. "Well, is anything missing?"

"She had a signed copy of *Tom Sawyer* she found at a garage sale last week I can't find nowhere. She was looking it up on the Internet to see what it was worth when I left her."

"That must be worth thousands?" Paula asked.

"Yeah, but that's all smoke. I know who did it, and it wasn't for no book."

Paula's eyes lit up. "Oh?"

"It's those old biddies we saw at a book-signing yesterday. One of them pretended to be some kind of Mark Twain expert, so she could find out where we live."

Paula touched the ear-bud that kept her in contact with her producer. "Thank you, Mr. Renfield. I need to switch back to the studio for more breaking news. This has been Paula Morgan reporting for Channel Three News."

"Well, at least we know his last name now," I said, hitting the mute button. Instead of breaking news, they went to a commercial. How putting a man and woman in two separate bathtubs will cure ED I didn't need to know.

"Did you hear that, Jake? He's accusing me and Patty of killing her!"

Her raised voice woke Fred, who had slept through the television broadcast. He moved closer to the door while I got up for more coffee.

Bonnie seemed to be preoccupied looking around the room when I refilled her cup. "Have you seen my purse?" she asked.

"On the counter by the fridge," I answered.

She got up and went over to her purse. "We would never hurt anyone. Why would he say it was us?"

Now Fred wanted out, making me get up again. "Who better to blame than someone with a motive," I answered while patting my dog on the head before opening the door.

Bonnie stopped fumbling through her purse and looked up at me in horror. "You think I did it, too?" I thought she was going to cry. Julie once said I should duct tape my mouth before speaking, and this time I had to agree.

"Of course not, Bon," I answered, trying to think of something to stop the tears before they started. "It's obviously that nasty boyfriend of hers. The way he spoke to her, and the bruise she had on her face at the signing, proves he doesn't think much of women. He probably lost his temper arguing over something, grabbed the file, and then stabbed her with it. Now he's trying to make it look like you and Patty did it. You've got to admit, the nail file was a brilliant touch."

"My God, Jake! It's gone!"

"What's gone, Bon?"

"My manicure kit. I always keep it on top of my purse where I can get to it. It's not here, Jake. You don't suppose..."

I finished for her. "That Craig took it and is framing you? No, he doesn't strike me as the kind who would plan that far ahead. His kind kills out of rage. I'm sure you misplaced it somewhere."

She came back to the table and resumed stirring her coffee. "Well, I hope you're right. My prints are all over the file."

I hoped I was right too. If it her nail file, she would have the means, as well as motive, to kill Shelia. The only thing missing for a conviction was opportunity, and I wasn't so sure she didn't have that too.

CHAPTER TWO

Shelia's murder all but vanished from the media's radar; marijuana sales still trumped local news stories, and Shelia was soon forgotten. Nearly a week had passed since Fred and I stopped at Bonnie's for morning coffee. A contractor I did odd jobs for had called and offered me a few weeks work hanging drywall in a house he was building in Bailey. As much as I hate drywall, it would pay the bills for a while.

It wasn't until Friday that Fred and I saw Bonnie again. The drywall job was finished for the week, and I had been paid in cash. I stopped off at Beau Jo's for a large Mountain Pie, with pineapple and pepperoni, after picking up some groceries at Safeway before heading home. It wasn't my favorite pizza, even Fred wouldn't eat the pineapple, but I knew Bonnie loved it. We could pick out the sweet fruit and give it to her.

We had just pulled into my driveway when I saw a truck racing down the road. I didn't think much of it and let Fred out. We were isolated, but not so that we didn't get the occasional lost driver now and then. I'd never known Fred to chase cars, so I was quite surprised when he ran after the truck, barking. The truck was much faster than Fred, and left him in a cloud of dust. But Fred was smarter. He left the road and ran down the hill, knowing the truck would have to pass by Bonnie's on the way out. That's when I noticed my front door wide open.

Whoever had been in there must have heard us coming up the road and got out before we pulled in. I put the pizza and groceries on the ground and ran after Fred. I made it to the lower road just in time to see a beat-up F150 come barreling down on him. It was the sleeveless guy from the book signing. He had no intentions of swerving to miss my dog. Luckily, Fred had no intentions of becoming road kill, and he jumped out of the way a second before the truck could run him over. But it wasn't in his nature to quit so quickly and he took off after the truck again. This time there were no shortcuts; he gave up the chase in less than twenty yards and came back panting to sit by my side.

I knelt down to hold his head and rub his ears. "It's okay, boy. You're lucky you didn't catch him. Don't you know you're no match for a speeding truck?"

"My, God, Jake! What's going on?" Bonnie was standing on her front deck with a towel wrapped around her head and lipstick smeared on her face. I took one look at Bonnie, and for a moment forgot about Sleeveless, then started laughing.

She looked at me like I'd lost my mind. "What's so damn funny? That guy could have killed Fred."

"Sorry, Bon, but I think you better go and finish your makeup."

She raised a hand to her face and felt her lipstick. "I must look a sight," she said with a giggle.

"Not if you plan on joining a circus." Her hand must have slipped when she heard all the commotion. She had a lopsided smile any clown would envy.

Fred might have laughed too if he had a sense of humor; then again, maybe he did because he started barking for no apparent reason. "I need to check on my house, Bon. Why don't you finish putting on your face and drive on up? I got your favorite pizza from Beau Jo's. I'll tell you why Fred was chasing the truck while we eat." I didn't wait for her to answer and started up the hill with Fred glued to my heels.

My cabin is built on a walkout foundation on a steep hill. I hadn't noticed the lower door on the way down, but did coming back. It was on the ground in pieces. Bonnie must not have heard Sleeveless making firewood of my door when she was in the shower. I had installed a reinforced deadbolt that was supposed to prevent this sort of break-in. Evidently, Sleeveless didn't read the promo for the lock.

Fred waited for me to enter before following. The big sissy wasn't so brave now that there wasn't a truck between him and whatever danger lay inside. Of course, there wasn't any danger once we stepped past the broken door, just a huge mess. The lower level was my office, my sanctuary from the world, where I kept my collection of first editions in built-in bookshelves lining the walls. My prized collection wasn't on those shelves; it was on the floor. I knew without the help of psychic powers that the copy of *Tom Sawyer* given to me by Julie would be missing. I didn't care if it was the key to a lost fortune or not. I had to get the book back. Julie had bought it for me when were strolling along Miner Street in Idaho Springs last year. I asked her to marry me the very next day.

"Okay, buddy, how about we go upstairs to see if he trashed that too?"

Bonnie was pulling into the driveway by the time we made it to the upper level. My cabin is small, less than eight hundred square feet, with one bedroom, a bathroom with a shower, but no tub, and a living room slash kitchen. The layout made it possible to see the road and driveway from almost any angle. My front door was wide open, but intact. Everything else looked to be as I had left it. I assumed the intruder must not have had time to search upstairs before Fred started barking, but like most assumptions, I was wrong.

I didn't bother to close the door on my way to inspect the bedroom. Bonnie would let herself in, and I really needed to check my shotgun. I had to smile when I saw my fierce guard dog wagging his tail when he saw Bonnie. Fifteen minutes ago, the scent of the intruder had his hair up and tail between his legs; now that the danger was over, he acted like nothing had happened.

The gun was gone, and so was the box where I kept Julie's wedding ring. I had kept them in a cedar chest at the foot of my bed with the gun on top where I could get to it in a hurry if any bears came knocking. Sleeveless had to search for the coins, for they were hidden at the bottom of the chest under a pile of family pictures and blankets.

"Anything missing?" Bonnie asked when she came in with my grocery bags.

"My shotgun and a cigar box where I kept Julie's ring and some silver quarters," I answered. Her lipstick was no longer smeared, but she must have fixed it quickly to get here so quickly, and it showed. I was in no mood to laugh this time. "Could you put those bags in the kitchen for me, Bon? I'll go out and get the pizza."

"Don't bother, Jake. It looks like some critter beat you to it. What little's left is covered in dirt."

Hoping I'd heard wrong, I looked outside toward my Jeep and saw the open pizza box and a few slices spread across my drive. "Damn, and it was your favorite."

Bonnie acted shocked at my outburst; I guess she wasn't used to me swearing. "I'll clean it up for you when I leave so Fred doesn't eat it. I know how much he loves pizza, but he might eat a rock, too," she said from the kitchen where she was already putting my groceries away.

I shut the door so Fred couldn't get to the pizza before Bonnie left, then went to help her before she decided to do my dishes, too. "Thanks, Bon, but I'll finish putting those away after I call in the burglary. We were going to surprise you. I even bought some honey for you to put on the crust."

I looked over in time to see her wipe a tear from her eyes. "You're such a sweet boy. I wish Diane had lived long enough to meet you. I'm sure you two would have fallen for each other, and I'd have the best grand-babies ever."

It was my turn to be uncomfortable, so I quickly changed the subject and looked away. "Did you get a look at the guy driving that truck? I think it was that tough-looking guy from the book signing."

She went back to unpacking my groceries. "The one ready to fight Shelia's boyfriend?"

I turned to Fred, who had been watching Bonnie, I suppose on the chance she'd drop something good to eat. "I think so. What do you think, Freddie?"

Bonnie answered for him. "Then he must have been looking for your copy of *Tom Sawyer* when he took your cigar box and gun."

"My, Fred, what a strange voice you have," I said.

Bonnie raised the corner of her lip, giving me a scowl I hadn't seen since Elvis made movies. "Funny,

Jake," she said and went back to rearranging my refrigerator.

Realizing she wasn't going to quit until everything was put away, I walked over to the table where I had left my phone and keys. "Sorry, but it sure looked like him. How many bald guys do you know running around in shirts without sleeves?"

She smiled while making a display of counting on her fingers. "Well, there's Kojak, and then that *Star Trek* captain, what's his name? But I don't remember any of them wearing tank-tops."

"Jean-Luc Picard," I answered. "But who the heck is Kojak?"

"Before your time, sonny," she said and laughed. "Okay, so it's the bald guy from the bookstore."

"And he wasn't wearing a tank-top. It was a denim shirt with the sleeves cut off," I replied, mimicking her turned-up lip. "At least now he can go out and buy a decent shirt with the money he stole."

"How much did he get, Jake?"

"Oh, it wasn't much. Only twenty-five bucks in face value; I don't know what they'd be worth in silver. I can live without the coins, it's the ring and book I'll miss. Well, the shotgun too. My father died shortly after giving me the gun, and I never had a chance to tell him how much he meant to me. I've got to find that SOB, Bonnie. He took the three things that mean the most to me."

As if he understood, Fred squeezed by Bonnie and sat at my feet. "Except for you, old boy," I said, patting him on the head with one hand, and picking up my cell with the other. "I better call the sheriff from my deck, Bon. My cell doesn't work so well in the house."

Bonnie stayed inside waiting for the coffee while I made my call. My back deck is right off the kitchen area and sits ten feet off the ground with a view of snowcapped Mount Evans. Fred stayed with Bonnie, I assume because she was closer to the refrigerator than me. I didn't close the door when I went out. Except for the occasional fly, mosquitoes and other flying bugs weren't a problem this high up, so Fred could join me when he was ready. I also knew it would save time rehashing my conversation with the sheriff because Bonnie would be able to hear everything I said.

"This is an emergency. Someone broke into my house," I told the operator just as Fred decided to join me. "Okay, give me the number, please."

I let the operator rattle off the telephone number for the sheriff's business line, knowing full well I wouldn't remember it because I had nothing at hand to write it down. "Yes, ma'am, I'll call it first thing Monday. Yes, thank you, too."

Bonnie appeared with coffee and some old donuts I had forgotten about as I finished my call. "They're not coming, are they?" she asked, handing me my cup.

"Not today. Maybe I'll go run a red light or something. Bet I get their attention then." I answered, trying to remember when I bought those donuts.

She dunked one of the donuts in her coffee. "Surely they don't expect you to leave everything until they get around to coming out here?" She took one bite, made a sour face, and threw the rest to Fred. He gulped it down and sat waiting for more. Then I remembered Julie had bought them last year.

"I don't know what they think, Bon, but I can't leave my house wide open while I wait for them. That door is an invitation for all the critters up here. Now that they've had a taste of Beau Jo's pizza, I'm sure they'll be back," I said while reaching for the donut bag so I could put it on the deck rail before Fred helped himself to more.

Bonnie swirled the coffee in her mouth before swallowing it. "Hold everything, Jake. I need something stronger to get this taste out of my mouth. I'll be right back."

She no sooner left us when a squirrel she called Chatter jumped out of the big spruce next to my deck, heading toward the donuts. Fred was after him in an instant. Fred was quick, but Chatter was quicker and jumped to the safety of the tree where he let Fred know he wasn't going anywhere. "Where was that squirrel when Sleeveless was here?" I asked Fred, between laughs. "He makes enough racket to scare off Satan himself."

"Sleeveless?" Bonnie had come back during all the commotion. "Oh, I get it, the burglar." She was all smiles now that she had her Jack Daniels.

I made a mental note to tell her it was illegal to carry an open bottle of booze in her car. "Yeah, and speaking of the devil, Bon, I've seen that guy somewhere. I wish I could remember where."

"I don't imagine it was in one of those fancy office buildings you used to work in. He looks more like a construction worker than a programmer," Bonnie paused long enough to pour some whiskey into her coffee. "Want a shot, Jake?"

"Tempting after what I've been through today, but no thanks. I need to go into town for a new door in a bit. It'd be my luck I'd get stopped by a cop."

She gave me her Elvis look again. "One little drink won't get you drunk," she said before her phone started ringing.

Bonnie looked at the caller ID before answering it. "Margot, I've been meaning to call you. Did you hear about Shelia?"

Margot is Bonnie's twin sister, and I knew she would be on the phone for some time. It was my chance to leave, so I whispered for Bonnie to let herself out and I'd catch her later.

The drive to the building supply store on the other side of town gave me time to reflect on my life and my decision to turn down a good-paying programming job. I thought that was all behind me until Bonnie had brought it up with her remark about Sleeveless. After I married Julie, I managed to find work at as a web developer and my soon to be manager agreed to let me work at home, which would allow me to take care of Julie who was recovering from Hodgkin's. But then the company reorganized before I could start work. My new boss, who wasn't much older than my daughter, was too much of a micro-manager to allow anyone to telecommute. I quit the job before it even began, and told him where he could put his new MBA.

I met Julie the previous summer when she had been investigating a rash of bear and elk poaching in the hills behind my home. She was so cute with her red ponytail sticking out the back of her warden's cap that I fell for her before she even spoke. She saved me from being arrested that day when she and her team found a planted compound-bow in my motor home. Julie noticed I was left-handed, and the bow was made for a right-handed person. My vision still gets blurry whenever I think of her.

Fred tired of catching bugs, or whatever it is dogs do when they stick their head out of an open car window, and put his head on my lap. I didn't have the heart to push him away, even though he would soon be drooling on my leg. I couldn't help but wonder if he was thinking of Julie too, when my cell phone rang. It was all I could do to get Fred off my lap and pull the phone out of my pocket; I nearly sideswiped the car next to me.

The other driver honked her horn and showed me her middle finger before I finally managed to turn on my phone. It was Bonnie.

"Jake! Thank God I got you. The cops are here asking a bunch of questions."

"They came anyway?" I asked, waving to the girl who had just saluted me. "The nine-eleven operator acted like I was bothering her."

"No! Not the sheriff, Jake. It's a couple homicide detectives."

I made a quick U-turn and headed back home.

"So where are they?" I asked as I jumped out of my Jeep after parking it in her driveway.

Bonnie was sitting in one of the rocking chairs on her front porch that I had made a few years back, during my craftsman phase. Even from a distance I could see she had been crying. With the way her makeup had stained her face, she looked like an ad for a zombie movie. "You're too late, Jake," she answered before starting to cry again. "They think *I* killed her. I thought they were going to arrest me."

Suspecting Bonnie of killing Shelia was no big surprise. Shelia's boyfriend, Craig, had said as much on live TV, and Bonnie did have a motive. I know I wouldn't think twice about lethal injection if someone killed *my* daughter.

I sat down in the rocker next to her. "It's okay, Bon. You have an alibi for the night of the murder. Me and Fred will vouch for you."

Fred looked up and barked at the mention of his name. He knew Bonnie was upset and laid down by her feet with his head on his paws.

"Would you do that for me, Freddie?" She asked, with the hint of a smile.

"You can bet your next pension check on it," I answered for my speech impaired dog, silently praying it didn't come to that. I wasn't in the habit of perjuring myself, nor was Fred.

Her smile had become a certified grin. "My, what a strange voice you have, Fred."

It made me smile too. "I guess I deserved that, but tell me what the cops said to you. We may have to find you a lawyer, *muy pronto*."

Although Fred and I were on the wagon, Bonnie wasn't. We ended up going to her kitchen where she kept her stock of whiskey. Her memory wasn't very clear by the time she finished a half-full fifth of Jack Daniels, but she did manage to tell me the story as best as she could remember.

The detectives played the good-cop, bad-cop routine on her in an effort to get her to confess to

Shelia's murder. The cops weren't buying the sweet, old-lady routine; not after Craig had told them how Bonnie had tried to murder Shelia's husband last year with peanut oil when she thought he was the hit-and-run driver. It was all the detectives needed to hear, even though spraying someone allergic to peanuts with Bactine mixed with peanut oil on a burn had as much effect as trying to kill ants with a water hose. They knew she was capable of murder, as did everyone else. But they didn't take into account that Shelia had met a violent death. She had been stabbed, which wasn't Bonnie's style. Bonnie would have used poison, or something that didn't involve blood.

She tried to tell the cops about how Craig beat Shelia, and that he should be their number-one suspect, but they weren't interested. They didn't quit badgering her until she'd said she needed a lawyer.

I waited for her to regain her composure with the help of Mr. Daniels. "I don't think it was Craig anyway, Bon."

"Of course it was him. Who else could it be?"

"Think about it, Bon. Craig told the television reporter he had been watching the CU game with a friend, and found Shelia dead on his return home. Craig is a mean SOB, but he doesn't strike me as dumb. He must know the cops will check out his alibi, so it only follows that someone else killed Shelia. My guess is she was killed for her copy of the book, and when it failed to be the key copy, the murderer went looking for another — mine."

The evening sun illuminated every wrinkle in her sixty-nine-year-old face. "The bald guy with tattoos and no sleeves? The guy who broke into your house?"

That was when I decided to find Shelia's killer. It was bad enough the guy stole my copy of *Tom Sawyer* and trashed my house, but I couldn't let them pin a murder on this old widow. I had to get him before the district attorney decided to go after her.

CHAPTER THREE

Between Bonnie's television and Fred barking at the top of the stairs whenever he thought he heard a critter in the lower level, I had a hard time concentrating on how to find Sleeveless. I should have closed the windows to silence her television, but air conditioning isn't necessary this high up and I needed the cool night air to cool the house or it would be too warm the next day.

It wasn't until the next morning that my plan started to come together. We were on our way to the building-supply store again before a family of skunks, or some other unwelcome visitors, decided the downstairs busted door was an open invitation to make themselves at home. What little traffic we encountered was in the opposite direction, weekend tourists headed to the lake, which gave me time to think without exercising the defensive driving skills required in Denver.

The plan was simple. On Monday, I would stop at the bookstore on my way home from the job in Bailey and try to get a list of the people who had been at the reading. I remember signing a guest register of sorts, so I could only hope Sleeveless did too. It wouldn't be easy, but once I eliminated the feminine names and everyone I knew, I should narrow the list down to less than a half dozen. But checking even five or six names could be tedious.

Most online searches can yield an address, phone number, and even relatives, but other than the social-media sites, none that I knew of displayed pictures. Somehow, Sleeveless didn't strike me as a social person. It would be tough to put a face to a name without a picture, especially a face I'd only seen for less than a minute.

His tattoo suggested he might have been a Marine at one time, so I could probably search the Department of Veterans Affairs database, or the National Personnel Records, but the paperwork to do so would take months. Fortunately, there are online sites that have instant access to those databases. Only they could be costly, so I'd have to narrow my list down to one or two names before I paid for one of those services. But where did I know him from? It had to be on a construction site unless he was one of those weekend bikers who wore a business suit the rest of the week. Anything was possible.

On the other hand, Sleeveless fit the classic profile of an ex-con: bald, tattooed and a build only obtained from having spent endless hours lifting weights, or maybe he cheated and took steroids. Maybe an online background check would work; but then again, maybe I'd seen too many Stallone and Schwarzenegger movies.

Fred woke me from my thoughts with an "I'm hungry" bark when we pulled into the parking lot of the building-supply store. His favorite fast-food restaurant was right next door. "Not today, Freddie. Julie might be watching." It was another bad habit she'd made us promise to quit.

It would have been torture to leave him in the Jeep in sight of those golden arches, so I put him on his leash and brought him with me. Evergreen's version of the national big-box store was half the size of its cousins in the Denver area. It was also pet-friendly, which saved me from pretending I was half blind and he was my service dog.

We had picked out a pre-hung, steel-clad entry door and were looking at some new deadbolts when Fred began to growl. I looked up just in time to see Sleeveless over in the roofing section. "Hush, Freddie," I whispered, trying to become invisible so I could follow Sleeveless back to his truck and get a license number. I was too late. He heard Fred, looked over at us, and froze like a cat stalking a bird. It was only a second or less, but long enough to feel the air temperature drop several degrees. For a moment our eyes locked on each other, then he picked up a gallon can of roofing cement, and threw it at us before he took off running.

The projectile missed us and hit the cart I had been pushing, creating a huge dent in my new door before it broke open and spilled its black, gooey tar all over the door and floor. I didn't see the glob on the floor, and slipped in the mess when I tried to give pursuit. Fred had been on the other side of the cart, so he missed stepping in it and managed to drag me another ten feet before giving up the chase. All I needed to complete my humiliation was a bag of feathers. I was covered from head to foot in tar.

"What the hell is going on here?" I looked up to see a huge figure clad in khaki colored pants, and wearing a white dress shirt. His nametag said Robert something, with *Manager* in big, bold letters. Before I could answer, several orange shirted employees started to gather. "I've already called the sheriff on the perp, Bob," one of them answered. She was an older woman, heavy set, and looked to be in her mid-fifties. I wasn't too sure about her age, for she lacked any makeup, and had really short hair. Sitting there on the floor, I had a great view of her hiking boots and a feeling she wouldn't mind planting one in my face if I tried to get up.

Fred came over to sit by me as the crowd grew bigger. I put my arm around him just in case someone tried to take him from me. "Maybe you should have called an ambulance instead," I said, without taking my eyes off the boots. "I hope your insurance is paid up." I had no intention of suing, and hadn't even thought about it until I realized I might be in trouble.

The manager's attitude changed faster than a politician at a news conference. "I'm sorry, sir, are you hurt?"

I slowly got to my feet, making a horrible face and holding my lower back. "Just bruised, I think. You really should be more careful who you let in your store. The guy who threw that can at me, must be some kind of maniac."

"Someone threw roofing cement at you?" By the tone of his voice, no one would suspect that only moments before he had been angry enough to swear.

Boots answered before I could. "That's why I called the sheriff, Bob. I thought they were fighting."

"Fighting! Fred and I were minding our own business when that psycho came out of nowhere and threw the can at us. Surely your cameras must have caught it."

"Fred? Who's Fred?" Bob's tone suggested he'd given up politics and gone back to being a manager.

Before I or anyone else could answer, I saw two deputies approach. One had a microphone he was talking into and the other was watching me with a hand on his holster.

"Negative on that ten-ten," said the cop on the mike, and then slipped the mike on a shoulder strap.

He was older and shorter than his partner, but with three stripes on his sleeve, I assumed he was the boss.

"Who's in charge here?" he asked.

"I am, Sergeant, but everything is under control now," Bob replied. Then turning to his employees, he said, "Don't you people have something to do?"

Boots was the last to leave; she gave me a look that suggested she'd like to meet me out in the alley, and I knew it wasn't to whisper sweet nothings in my ear.

"We got a call on a fight in progress. Is anyone hurt?" the sergeant asked.

"It wasn't a fight, Officer," I answered, holding Fred even tighter. "Some maniac threw a can of roofing tar at me and then ran out of here. I tried to catch him and slipped on this mess," I said, pointing to the floor.

The sergeant looked briefly at the tar on the floor before turning back to me. "That sounds like a fight to me. Can I see some identification?"

He took my driver's license then handed it to his partner. "Run this for me, Brandon, while I talk to the manager."

The sergeant took Bob aside while Deputy Brandon talked into his microphone, reading my name, address, birthday, physical attributes, and driver's license number to whoever was on the other end. I'm surprised he didn't mention my donor status too. In the meantime, I could barely hear what the sergeant and Bob were discussing. Although I missed most of it, I did hear Bob say something about Fred and lawyers.

All I could do was stand there holding Fred's leash, and wonder if I'd be asked to pay for the damaged door and cleanup costs. I didn't have to think about it for long before a page came over the loudspeaker asking for a manager. I saw the sergeant hand the manager a card, and then walk over to his partner. After a few words that I couldn't hear, they both came over to me.

Sarge did all the talking. "The management isn't going to press any charges at this time so you are free to go after a few more questions, Mr. Martin," he said, handing me my license back.

I started to ask, "Why would he press charges?" but bit my tongue and nodded okay instead.

"First off, who is Fred? Was somebody else with you?"

"Fred, give this nice officer a handshake and introduce yourself," I said.

The sergeant cracked a smile when Fred sat and offered his paw. "Well, aren't you a smart doggy?" he said before turning back to me. "What can you tell me about this man who assaulted you? Do you know him and why he would want to hurt you?"

"I believe he's the one who broke into my home."

"You had a burglary?"

"Last Friday." Officer Brandon said before I could. "According to dispatch, he reported a break-in and a missing shotgun."

"Not to mention a rare book, some silver coins and a gold ring," I added.

The sergeant looked annoyed. I assumed because his partner didn't tell him sooner, but then for all I knew it might be his lunch hour and I was keeping him from visiting Fred's favorite restaurant next door. "So you *do* know the suspect?" he asked, pulling out a small notebook and pen from his shirt pocket.

"Not really. I saw him at a book signing a week ago Friday, the same night Shelia Dean was killed."

He stopped writing and looked up, pointing his pen at me. "Shelia who?"

Deputy Brandon answered for me again. I was ready to ask if they wouldn't mind me leaving so they could interrogate each other. "The Nail File Murder, sir. The one in Lakewood."

The sergeant didn't seem to catch on. Either that or he missed his calling, for he had a poker face that showed nothing. "And you think they're connected? This Shelia who was murdered with a nail file and your burglar?"

Fred had tired of the interview and let me know by pacing back and forth. Luckily we weren't in the garden section or he would be looking for a tree. "Yes, I think so. It's all in a report my neighbor gave to your detectives. I hope you don't mind, but my dog needs to relieve himself."

Sarge looked down at Fred then put his notebook back in his pocket. "Okay, thank you for your statement, Mr. Martin, and the manager would like to talk to you after you take care of your dog."

Sleeveless was long gone by the time we left the store, but at least I had a new door and deadbolt at a huge discount. Just mention a lawsuit and everything changes.

By Monday, my well-thought-out plan of finding Sleeveless from a list of names and comparing them to known felons had changed now that I knew a better way to track him down. I had spent Sunday afternoon fixing my door when an epiphany came to me. All I really needed was access to the video tapes from the building-supply store. Chances were pretty good Sleeveless would be seen running to his truck, and with a little luck, we would have its license plate to track him down.

Bonnie took all of five minutes, over our morning cup of coffee, to blow holes in my epiphany. "And how do you plan on seeing those tapes?" It felt like the time my fifth-grade teacher pointed out all the mistakes in my first, and last, attempt to write poetry. "It's not like it's a mom and pop store, Jake. They probably have more rules and procedures to follow than the clerks at the DMV. That manager isn't going to let you have those tapes unless you get a court order."

She refilled my coffee and smiled. "But your first plan might work. Except for a couple of little things, it was a good plan."

"Thank you, Miss Henson. Can I go out and play now?"

Bonnie quit filling her cup and looked up. She had several new wrinkles I hadn't noticed before. I stopped her before she could speak. "My fifth-grade teacher, Bon. For a moment there you reminded me of her."

The wrinkles faded and I swear I saw a twinkle in her blue eyes. "Did you know I used to be a teacher? I subbed before Diane was born. You could have been one of my students if you had lived here at the time."

"I'm sorry my dog ate my homework, ma'am, but if you give me another chance, I promise I'll come up with a better plan."

Bonnie continued the game and looked over at Fred, who had gone back to sleep some time ago, presumably after he realized there would be no breakfast. "Did you eat Jake's homework, Freddie?"

Fred raised his head at the mention of his name, but when no table scraps appeared, he went back to sleep.

"Seriously, Bon, what's wrong with my plan?"

She got back up from the table and headed toward the sink with her coffee pot. "Well, to begin with, that list of names. It's usually the author who collects those names so you would have to get the list from him. Paul Wilson ain't from around these parts, pilgrim, so that won't be no easy chore."

She paused to rinse out the pot while I waited for her to continue. "You want me to make more coffee?" she asked, turning back toward me.

"No thanks, Bon. So what else? You said a couple of things were wrong with my plan."

She didn't answer at first. She reminded me so much of my mother the way she stared at nothing at all, looking confused. "Huh? Oh my, I seem to have forgotten. It's probably not that important, whatever it was."

My text-message tone interrupted any further conversation. It was the first time the annoying beep didn't bother me. "Looks like I better get over to Bailey before they get someone else to hang the drywall. Just the same, if you can call down to the bookstore and see if they have the list or know how to contact the author, I'll get on it as soon as I get back. I'll hang a few sheets then make some excuse to quit early. It shouldn't take me more than a couple of hours."

Those couple hours turned into most of the day, and I didn't even get my hands dirty, at least not hanging drywall. I was laid off before I got started; replaced by some day-laborers the contractor picked up in town whose English was questionable but willing to work for half my pay. My old Wagoneer broke down on the way home, somewhere between Conifer and Evergreen. I tried calling Bonnie, only to find the narrow valley was a cell phone dead zone. When my thumb failed to get Fred and I a ride, we walked at least a mile back toward Highway 285 until I could pick up a signal.

Bonnie didn't answer her home phone, so I tried her cell thinking that she might be at the bookstore getting the list of names I asked for. I got the same result, and left her a message telling her about my predicament. She was the only neighbor or friend that I could ask for help. I hardly knew any of my other neighbors, let alone their names or numbers. It left me with no choice but to call triple A and use my last tow of the year.

Bonnie was waiting with her hands on her hips when the tow-truck driver finally pulled into my drive several hours later. She must have seen us coming and drove her Cherokee up the east loop of the circle, beating the slower tow truck.

Fred wasted no time hopping out of the truck and running over to greet her. You'd think he hadn't seen her in ages the way he acted. His tail was wagging back and forth faster than a bobble-head doll on a rough road.

Bonnie left Fred and came over to me while I was signing the driver's paperwork. "I tried to call you back, Jake. Is your phone working?"

I thanked the driver then turned toward Bonnie. Fred had already forgotten her and gone on to check out a tree. "Guess you get what you pay for, Bon. This new phone doesn't seem to work very well up here, but it does wonders for getting me some exercise."

She didn't get the joke, not knowing I had to walk a mile for service, and looked at me like I was the bulb on the Christmas tree that made all the lights go out. I waited for the tow-truck driver to leave before explaining what had happened.

"You either need to get a new car, Jake, or a new phone. You could have been murdered trying to hitchhike." She sounded like my mother did the first time I hitched a ride.

I ignored her comment. I couldn't afford a new phone, let alone a new car, and didn't want to talk about my finances. "I think it's the fuel pump this time. Do you mind giving us a ride to the parts store before they close?"

We were on the part of our road known as dead man's curve when I realized my mistake of asking for a ride and double checked my seat belt. "Are you okay, Bon?" I asked right after she came within inches of going off the road.

She answered without looking at me. "Of course I am. Just got a little distracted thinking about that list you asked me to get is all."

I wanted to ask if she'd been drinking, but the fear in her eyes convinced me she was sober. The close call had startled her more than me, so I let it go.

I waited until we were off the hill and nearly in town before pursuing my thoughts. "Is Sleeveless on the list?"

It took a moment for my question to register, perhaps because we hadn't spoken since she mentioned the list. "Oh, Appleton. I doubt it. Jackie gave me the list of people she had invited to the signing. The author kept the guest register. But isn't that better? I mean some people never sign those registers. I know I don't. Well, maybe at a funeral service, but for the most part, I just ignore them. Like those guest registers at all the welcome stations you see across the country. You know when you cross a state line. It's really none of their damn business where I'm from or where I'm going. You ask me, it's just another way for Big Brother to keep track of us."

Now I knew she had been drinking. She tended to babble on about nothing when she got together with Jack Daniels. I would have to find a way to get her keys on the ride back. "You're forgetting about the flyers and the ad in the paper, Bon. Remember how upset Craig was when he claimed the paper said Wilson was supposed to tell where to find hidden treasure, and he demanded that Wilson get to the point? I'll bet Fred's next meal that's how Sleeveless found out about the event. Something tells me he wouldn't be on any book-club reading list."

"Well, you can check for yourself. Its right here somewhere," she said, taking her eyes off the road to rummage through her purse.

I grabbed the wheel just in time to save a head-on when she drifted into the oncoming lane. I would have had her pull over then and there to let me drive, but we were already at the auto parts store. Bonnie would have made NASCAR proud; she did the twenty-minute drive in just under ten minutes.

The argument over me driving home never happened. Bonnie had stayed in the car with Fred, and I found her in the passenger seat after leaving the auto-parts store. A State Patrol car, that wasn't there when we pulled in, was parked next to us with no one in it.

"Maybe you better drive, Jake," she said when she saw me. I later found out that she had nearly wet her pants until she saw the cop go into a nearby coffee shop.

The sun had gone down behind Mount Evans creating an eerie, red glow by the time the three of us made it back to Bonnie's. Fred and I left after making sure she got into her house safely, and then we hurried up the trail to our cabin before it was too dark to see. I couldn't wait to start checking on the list Bonnie gave me. It was the best lead I had to get a name and address for Sleeveless.

After feeding Fred and throwing a frozen pizza in the microwave oven for myself, I sat down to begin my search. I started by eliminating feminine names. Not because I'm a chauvinist like my ex called me, but because a guy with biceps that would put Hercules to shame probably didn't have a girl's name. There was the possibility he had a name like Robin, but I didn't see any of those on the list. There were at least ten pages of results for every name I had chosen from Bonnie's list. By the time I finished, I knew less than when I started.

Fred woke me somewhere around two or three in the morning. I had fallen asleep at the kitchen table while clicking through promising links during my search. He was pacing back and forth at the front door. I had forgotten to let him out to do his thing, and he couldn't hold it any longer. "Maybe I should trade you in for a cat. I hear they can be trained to use a toilet; some even know how to flush it when they're done."

He stopped pacing, laid down by the door with his head on his paws, and stared at me with the saddest brown eyes.

"You know I was just kidding, Freddie," I said, patting him on the head while opening the door. There was enough light from the waxing moon for me to watch him from the porch. I told myself I was checking for any nocturnal critters, but the truth is I was a little paranoid about someone lurking outside my cabin. There's something about having a home burglary that makes a person extra cautious. Fred must have been scared too. He finished his business and came back to the cabin in record time, but not before it dawned on me how to find Sleeveless.

CHAPTER FOUR

I had been searching all the wrong places. If Sleeveless was truly the crook I suspected, he undoubtedly had a record. I didn't have access to any criminal databases, but I remembered reading an article awhile back about some websites that published pictures of known felons and sex offenders, and in the case of sex offenders they even pinned their location on a map. The author of the article was trying to get these websites shutdown because she thought it was an invasion of their civil liberties.

After fifteen minutes of my renewed search, I found a rogues' gallery hosted by the Denver Post. Two hours later, I had a name and last known address for Sleeveless.

Thankfully, sleep came quickly once I lay down again. I was too tired to work out the details or devise a plan on what I should do next, but my subconscious wasn't. When I woke the next morning, I knew exactly what to do.

Once I heard the morning news blasting on Bonnie's television, Fred and I went down for coffee and to tell her I'd found Sleeveless, or as I knew him now, John Appleton of Pine Junction. I needed to borrow her Cherokee because my Jeep was still out of commission. The fuel pump I'd bought the day before could wait until I got Julie's ring and book back. The thought of breaking into his house to retrieve my property would have never crossed my conscious mind, but the subconscious didn't have the same principles and it couldn't wait until I fixed my Jeep.

"I'm going with you, Jake. You can drive if you want, but no way am I going to stay here while you go after the creep," Bonnie said after I told her why I wanted to borrow her Cherokee.

I wished I hadn't told her about Appleton. My subconscious didn't tell me she would want to come along. "Are you crazy, Bon? This guy is dangerous. He was arrested last year for armed robbery."

She walked over to the key-rack she kept next to her front door and removed her car keys. "It's my car and I go where it goes," she said, clutching them in her hand.

I felt like I was six again, arguing with my sister. "Bonnie, listen to me. I'm only asking to borrow your Cherokee because I don't have time to fix my Jeep right now. I need to make sure it's him before he goes to work, or whatever he does for a living." I failed to mention the part about breaking into his house.

"That's stupid, Jake. You just said how dangerous he is. Do you want him to shoot you with that gun he stole from you?"

"I'm not going to confront him. I'll park your Cherokee where it can't be seen from his house and walk back and hide behind a tree or something. Once I see it's him, I'll call the sheriff."

Her fingers relaxed their grip on the keys, but just when I thought she was going to hand them over, she reached for her purse and coat. "All the more reason why I'm going with you guys. You know your phone won't work over there. I promise I won't do anything stupid. I'll stay in the car with Fred and wait for you. I can be your backup and call 911 if something goes wrong."

"Great. A dog that can't catch squirrels and a sixty-nine-year-old granny covering my back. I'll be lucky to live long enough to see my own grandchildren." The words no sooner left my lips when I realized I'd said the wrong thing.

Bonnie's eyes dimmed, and she turned away. I'd forgotten how many times she had cried after a few too many drinks over the lost hope of grandkids. "I'm sorry, Bon. I suppose it won't hurt if you come along. You can even help by keeping my mutt quiet while I play hide and seek."

Appleton lived within walking distance of Pine Junction, but over the county line in a cabin smaller than mine. It looked like it was built back in the sixties or seventies before Park County had building codes. What had started as a three hundred square foot A-frame chalet had doubled in size over the years with the addition of a couple shed-dormers. The truck that had nearly run over Fred was parked in a dirt drive next to the east addition. I had taken all this in while slowly driving by the cabin. We had only seen one other vehicle since leaving highway 285, so I didn't worry about holding up traffic, but I was concerned the other driver might wonder why I was going so slowly.

"I hope he doesn't come back to check on us," I said aloud.

"Who, Jake?"

"The driver of that Datsun. You better keep an eye out for him when I go into the cabin. It shouldn't be hard to miss. I haven't seen one of those old pickups since I was a teenager," I said while pulling into Appleton's driveway.

Bonnie had her seatbelt off and her hand on the door lever before I came to a complete stop. "Where do you think you're going?" I asked. "Please do as you promised and stay here with Fred while I'm gone."

"He's bound to recognize you, Jake. I'll go and you two stay here. I can pretend I broke down, or have a flat tire or something, and ask to use his phone. Even an ex-con wouldn't hurt a little old lady. Would he?"

I put the Cherokee in gear and drove away. "Are you kidding, Bon? He must have seen you at the bookstore. I can't take the chance he'll remember you." What was I thinking? I didn't have a clue about what to do now that we'd found Sleeveless. This guy was a violent felon. Finding him had been a game of wits, safely played out on a computer without any possibility of a physical confrontation. Now it had suddenly turned deadly with the threat of meeting him face-to-face.

"Let's go back to the highway and wait at that little cafe. He has to pass it on his way out. Then we can come back here and I'll retrieve my stuff after he's gone." Too late, I realized I'd let my true intentions of coming here escape. I expected Bonnie to be shocked.

Bonnie's grin went from one ear to the next. "That's the best idea I've heard all day."

Fred jumped over the rear seat and ran to the back of the Cherokee. He barked when we passed Appleton's cabin then came back and put his big head on the top of the bench seat where we sat. I'm sure if he could talk he would let me know John Wayne wouldn't be running away. The Duke would have gone in there and beat Sleeveless to a pulp.

We didn't have to wait long. I was about to put Fred back in the Cherokee, after letting him circle a grassy knoll outside the cafe, when the beat-up F150 went sailing by. Bonnie saw it too and stopped just shy of entering the cafe. Ten minutes later, the three of us were back at Appleton's cabin.

Without the danger of being shot by my own gun, I parked where the F150 had been, and told my sidekicks to wait in the car. Bonnie wasn't in the habit of taking orders, and I didn't have the time to argue when she followed me to the door with Fred bringing up the rear. After knocking to make sure no one was inside, I went around to the front of the cabin with my entourage close behind. Like most A-frames built during its era, this one had a deck in the front with a sliding-glass door. It had been the main entrance before all the additions had been built. I checked to see if any neighbors could see us before we climbed the short flight of stairs onto the deck. Appleton's cabin was fairly secluded. The only other house I saw was several hundred yards down the road, and it looked empty.

My plan to get inside was simple. All I had to do was lift the sliding panel of the glass door. The flimsy locks they put on these early models were no deterrent to even a novice burglar. Not that I have a lot of practice breaking into homes; it was something I learned in my sideline as a handy-man. That plan went out the proverbial window when Bonnie noticed a blood stain on the deck and the slider wide open.

I've read enough murder mysteries to know we shouldn't go inside, but I could see my shotgun on the kitchen table. I had to get it and look for my ring and book before the cops took them for evidence, or I could forget about ever seeing them again. Fred solved that minor dilemma for me and went in without having to worry about disturbing evidence or being arrested for breaking and entering.

With his nose to the floor, he headed straight for the kitchen. Appleton either had dog food sitting in a bowl, or he'd left some other tasty morsel lying around.

"Hello? Anyone home?" Bonnie asked, sticking her head through to door while I was still wondering what to do if we found a body.

I scooted past Bonnie and went inside when Fred disappeared into one of the room additions. "Wait here, Bon. Fred smells something. It might not be something you want to see."

I grabbed my shotgun from the table, checked to see if it was loaded, and crept close to the wall as I approached the room Fred had gone into. I stopped just outside the open door and tried to listen. The only sound I heard was Bonnie's breathing. She had completely ignored my warning and was attached to me at the hip.

"You know he's not in there, Jake. We saw him drive by us in the truck. Why are you being so cautious?" she whispered. The problem was she whispered like she was at a rock concert.

I was about to give up the stealth attack and just barge into the room when Fred came moseying out with a sock in his mouth.

"Not now, boy," I said when he tried to put it in my hand and before I realized he didn't want to play tug-a-war. It wasn't a sock after all.

The first clue that it wasn't a sock was the texture. Unless Appleton was into wearing paper socks, Fred had brought me a crumpled up sheet of notebook paper.

"Blood sucking bug pass," I read aloud, without the fear of someone lurking behind the door. It would not have meant a thing if not for the numbers next to each word. I would check my copy of *Tom Sawyer* if I ever got it back, but I knew instantly Appleton had decoded Drake's enigma.

"What's *that* supposed to mean?" Bonnie asked, now that we had moved past the door and she had managed to detach herself from my side without surgery.

"I think it's the code telling where the old miner's treasure is hidden. It's a code within a code," I said, making a quick check of the room.

There was a single bed, a computer desk with the computer still on, and a dresser. They were all in the style of early Goodwill, worth a good fifty dollars at most.

"We better make it quick, Bon. He wouldn't leave the door open and his computer on if he was on the way to Mexico."

She walked over to look at the computer monitor as if she hadn't heard me. "Do you suppose he knows what the code means, Jake?" She quickly turned away with a disgusted look.

"Men. Is that all you guys ever think about?"

"No," I answered when I saw what was on the screen.

I reached over and turned off the monitor. "Right now I'm wondering what jail food tastes like. We better get out of here before someone shows up."

Bonnie had the top dresser drawer open before I finished talking. "Aren't you gonna look for your cigar box? Maybe it's in here. I'll…"

Fred cut her off with a short bark. I hadn't noticed he had gone back outside until he ran back in the room to get my attention. Then I heard the truck.

CHAPTER FIVE

Bonnie must have heard the truck, too, because stopped rifling through the dresser and looked up at me. Her eyes were huge. "My God, Jake, he's back!" She was holding a pair of Appleton's shorts, and any other time it would have been funny. She had an index finger poking out a hole meant for something else.

"Quick, Bon, close that drawer and let's go out on the deck. We'll pretend we never came inside." Bonnie didn't move. She was frozen in place and had turned whiter than fresh snow. I grabbed her by the arm and hurriedly led her outside before Appleton could catch us in his house.

Once outside, I realized it wouldn't take him ten seconds to find us out. It was time to take the offense. I opened the gun's breach to make sure it was still loaded, then snapped it shut. The double-barrel shotgun was an antique, but very effective with number-two buckshot at close range.

"Grab Fred's collar and get behind me when he comes up, Bon, but not too close; this gun has a pretty good kick." I cocked both hammers and waited.

The truck didn't move, and Appleton didn't get out. He just stayed there with the motor spewing blue-white smoke out the tailpipe. I couldn't actually see his face because of the glare on his dirty windshield. Was he on his phone calling the sheriff? Or worse, was he loading his own gun? What was he doing?

Fred didn't wait to find out, and took off down the deck stairs before Bonnie could catch his collar.

"Fred! No! Get back here! Now!" I might as well have been yelling at the trees.

Bonnie was back to being Bonnie. "Go get him, Freddie! Show him we mean business."

I didn't waste time with the stairs and vaulted over the rail. I wasn't about to let that creep hurt my dog. The drop from the deck to the ground was only a few feet, but I landed on a large rock and twisted my leg causing me to fall. The butt of the gun hit the ground hard and fired. Appleton put his truck in reverse and raced out the driveway before Fred could reach him. Fred knew from experience he couldn't catch the truck once it was on the road and gave up the chase. He was back with a huge grin on his face before I managed to get up.

"Good boy," Bonnie said, reaching down with both hands to rub his head. "You showed that pervert who's the boss." She had taken the slower, but safer, way to get off the deck by walking down the stairs.

"I still have some old Keystones in the fridge, if you want one, Jake," Bonnie said before taking a sip of her Jack Daniels. We were recalling our adventure while watching the sun slip behind Mount Evans from her back deck. If ever there was a time I needed a beer, it was now. I'm sure Fred could use one too, but I knew Julie was watching and we couldn't let her down.

"No thanks, Bon. I'll wait for the coffee." Fred had cold water he didn't drink. It would have been the quintessential Rocky Mountain spring night if not for her police scanner squawking in the background to remind me we had just committed a felony of breaking and entering.

Being a possible fugitive didn't seem to bother Bonnie. She was amazing. She hadn't cared one bit if Appleton called the sheriff; she had been hell-bent on going back inside to look for my cigar box. I had to talk myself silly to get her to leave his cabin before the law arrived, but I'm glad she was on my team. Though she didn't find it, I was amazed at her lack of fear.

Bonnie looked at the wrinkled paper again and took another sip of her drink. "Blood sucking bug pass. Do you think that's the location of the Tenderfoot, or where Drake stashed his gold?"

"Most likely the gold, if those numbers are the code he left for his niece to decode. I'll have to get a copy of Paul Wilson's book and verify them, but we still don't have a clue as to what it means."

"Patty has a copy, Jake. I'll ask to borrow it first thing in the morning." Bonnie had that little-girl gleam in her eye again, and I could tell it wasn't from her drink. "Oh, this is so exciting. We're going on a real treasure hunt."

"Whoa there, partner. Nobody said anything about searching for it. You won't be doing much treasure hunting from a jail cell. Let's concentrate on finding Shelia's killer first."

She put the paper down on the little deck-table before taking a long swallow from her glass. "We know who did it. We practically caught Sleeveless with his pants down."

I choked on my coffee. The vision of Bonnie with her finger sticking through Appleton's shorts and the image on his computer screen made me laugh before I could finish swallowing. "That's not the point, Bon. You and I both know he killed Shelia while stealing her copy of the book, and when he found it was the wrong copy, he helped himself to mine. The point is we can't prove any of it."

She paused with both hands around her glass, thinking about what I'd said. "It's all circumstantial, isn't it?"

Bonnie's police scanner cut me off before I could answer. She nearly dropped her drink when a dispatcher mentioned Appleton's name. He had been found dead in his truck. There was more, but I couldn't hear it over the static.

Bonnie went over to her scanner to silence its screeching, but not before we heard the mention of suicide. She turned to me with eyes the size of quarters. "Suicide?"

"That's what they said," I answered. "Kind of hard to believe, isn't it?"

"You don't suppose it was because he knew we figured out he killed Shelia?" she asked, now holding her glass tightly with both hands.

"He didn't seem like the kind to kill himself, Bon."

A vision of Appleton trying to run over my dog when Fred had chased his truck flashed through my mind. "What do you think, Fred? Do you smell something fishy?"

Fred didn't answer, but raised his head at the mention of his name. He had slept through the excitement of the scanner, and I felt bad for waking him from his dreams. For all I knew he might have caught Chatter, or met a pretty Collie. I reached down to rub his ears, but froze when the scanner came back on.

Bonnie managed to raise the volume in time for us to hear someone request a tow-truck at Three Sisters

Park to haul Appleton's truck away. "I think Fred and I might go there tomorrow, Bon."

"Three Sister's Park? What do you expect to find there?"

"Not the park, Bon. I want to go back to Appleton's cabin before they send out their forensics team. Our prints are all over the place."

She set her glass on the table next to the wrinkled paper from Appleton's bedroom. "Why would they do that? Are you saying he didn't kill himself?"

"You're forgetting the blood stain on the deck, Bon. I'm no expert, but it looked fresh and someone tried to wash it out. Maybe somebody was trying to make it look like suicide."

"Are you sure I can't get you a beer, Jake. It would help you think better. How did he drive back and catch us there if he'd already been killed? You gonna tell me he's a zombie?"

"Zombie or not, it doesn't smell right, and I'm sure the cops will smell it too."

I was torn between leaving Fred with Bonnie and taking him with me the following morning. Bonnie made the decision for me when she used the same tactic as the day before. My Jeep was still down and if I wanted to use her Cherokee, I had to take her along.

"Only if I drive," I told her, trying to look like I meant it. I used my mean face, the one I use when

Fred has done something bad, where I stare without blinking.

She wasn't buying it. "Should we let the little boy drive, Freddie?"

My mean voice had worked on him. He was at my side acting like a concrete statue, but managed a short bark when he heard her question.

"Okay, you guys win, but only because I need to fix my face and it will save time if I do it while you drive."

We drove past Appleton's slowly, but not slow enough to be suspicious if someone should be watching. Once satisfied that the cabin wasn't being watched, we went back and pulled into the drive. I parked close to the deck stairs instead of the front door. There was no need to clean the door of prints because we had entered through the sliding door on the deck.

I turned to Bonnie who had already unhooked her seat belt and was reaching for the door handle. "Bon, please don't," I said before she could open the door. "I need you to stay here with Fred and watch the road while I go in and wipe the place down."

"It's my prints too, Jake. I can't take the chance you'll miss anything."

"Please, Bon. You'll slow me down and I need you to be my lookout."

She let go of the door handle and sat back without saying a word. If I didn't know better, I'd swear she was pouting.

"I'm sorry, Bon Bon. I didn't mean to hurt your feelings. It's just that I really need you to watch my back."

A cigarette and lighter appeared from nowhere. "I'm not a cripple, Jake. Just because I'm old, doesn't mean I'm slow," she said, before flicking on her lighter.

The cabin looked the same as when we were here yesterday. I knew I had to be quick for it was only a matter of time before someone showed up, so I started at the sliding door then worked my way toward the bedroom, wiping everything we might have touched with a rag coated with lemon oil. I had seen on some TV show where prints couldn't be lifted from an oily surface. It sounded logical, whether it was true or not, but too late I realized how stupid I'd been. Maybe Bonnie should have come with me after all. I'm sure she would have known better.

Appleton had been a slob. The place looked like it hadn't been cleaned in months, so my attempt to wipe prints became all too obvious when I went to clean off the table where my shotgun had lain. I needed to wipe the whole table or even a rookie cop would see someone had tried to remove finger prints.

It would be like leaving little sticky notes saying 'look here'.

If only moving the clutter to clean under it was so simple. My brilliant idea to wear latex gloves was stupid, because they were now coated in lemon oil. I couldn't touch anything without staining it with oil from the gloves, and if I took them off, I'd be leaving more prints than I started with.

Appleton had inadvertently solved the problem for me. Among the mess on the table was a dirty dish towel. Using the towel as a makeshift pair of gloves, I could now move a stack of books that included Forrest Fenn's book and several overdue library books on lost Rocky Mountain treasures. There was also a Lakewood phone book and a printout on paper with holes punched on the sides. I was in still in high school the last time I saw that kind of paper; it had to be thirty years old, but wasn't. Thirty-year-old paper should be yellow with faded ink, and this looked like it was printed yesterday. A quick glance told me it was a copy of the Rocky Mountain News article Paul Wilson had mentioned at his book signing.

More clutter was stacked on top of a small tin box. My heart nearly stopped when I went to move the box heard the distinctive sound of coins. Sure that Julie's ring would be there, I tore off the top of the box, but all I found were my coins and a flash drive.

Where was her ring? Did he sell or hock it? I wanted to throw the tin box across the room, and probably would have if not for Fred. He was sitting on the other side of the table wearing a grin on his face.

"What are you doing here, Freddie?" The question was really meant for Bonnie, for she was standing behind him at the sliding-glass door.

"Jake, I think we better leave." Her wrinkled forehead and frown spelled worry.

"I'm almost finished, Bon. Give me another minute and I'll be right out."

"You don't have another minute. Someone has driven by a couple times in a fancy SUV, and I'm sure they saw my Cherokee."

"I can't leave yet, I'm not finished. Keep an eye out for me while I check the bedroom."

She surprised me when she didn't argue. I thought for sure she would have come in to help, or should I say snoop. Evidently, she took the SUV seriously.

I quickly finished with the table then had a brilliant idea. I put most of my coins and the flash drive in my pockets, but left a few quarters. Somewhere in my twisted logic, I thought the police wouldn't suspect anyone had been here when they saw the coins. Any self-respecting burglar wouldn't leave cash money behind.

Pleased with my clever subterfuge, I hurried to the bedroom door to wipe its frame and knobs, and anything Bonnie or I might have touched or leaned against. Two minutes later, I joined her at the door.

She pointed toward the kitchen. "You missed those paw prints by the fridge, Jake."

I followed her finger and saw where Fred had sniffed for food. There was no way I could clean those without doing the entire floor. "It's too late now. We'll leave the door open and hope they think a neighbor's dog made them."

She was gone when I turned back to the sliding door. I made one last wipe of the jamb where she had been resting her hand, and followed her to the car with Fred one step behind me. I couldn't help but wonder if the FBI kept track of dog prints.

Bonnie was behind the wheel, and I wanted to leave the scene of our crime quickly, so I didn't argue about her driving. "I think all we did was dig a deeper hole," I said while watching out the rear window for the mysterious SUV once we were back on the road.

She looked over at me as she turned onto 285. "Why's that, Jake?"

Suddenly, the blare of a semi truck's horn made us nearly jump out of our seats. Bonnie had cut off the big rig and it missed us by inches when its driver swerved into another lane.

I subconsciously crossed myself. "He's probably calling the sheriff this very minute."

She started pouting again. "He shouldn't be going so fast down this hill, and that's what I'll tell the sheriff if he does report me."

"Not the truck driver, Bon. The guy in the SUV. He's probably reporting us right now."

"Oh, him. Well, I doubt if he got a license number. That would have been impossible the way you parked next to the side entrance."

She was probably right and her Cherokee was as common in the foothills as pine beetles, so telling the cops what we were driving would narrow the suspect list down to a few hundred thousand. Still, it wouldn't take a Sherlock Holmes to track us down; even Inspector Clouseau would be able to do it in time.

We stopped at the lake in Evergreen before heading up the canyon to our homes. Fred had been cooped up too long, and needed to stretch his legs. Bonnie needed a cigarette to calm her nerves, and I needed to think.

"That was close, Bon," I said once we found a bench away from the lake house where Fred could water some trees.

She paused with her cigarette in midair. "I feel like a little girl again, Jake. That was fun."

"Are you sure your last name isn't Parker?"

"You've got to admit, Clyde, that was exciting," she answered before taking a deep drag.

She waited long enough to feel the nicotine then exhaled. "I'm sorry you didn't find your book or ring, but I'm glad you at least got your coins back."

Watching the smoke circle in front of her, she continued. "I would have never thought to look in that box. But you should have taken all of them. Your prints must be on the ones you left behind."

I had told her about finding my coins on our trip back from Pine Junction, and I couldn't resist mentioning how clever I'd been to leave a few behind. Leave it to Bonnie to burst my bubble.

Fred came back and sat by my feet, listening to every word we said. "All the more reason we need to find out who killed Appleton," I said.

Instinctively, I reached out to pet Fred. It was more for my comfort than his. "Now both of us will be murder suspects. They might take pity on a little old lady, but you can bet they'll throw me and Fred in jail first and ask questions later."

Bonnie started to say something, but coughed instead. Once she recovered, she flipped her cigarette into the lake. "You really think someone murdered Sleeveless?"

Fred lost interest in our conversation and went off to bark at some ducks in the water. I kept one eye on him while I answered Bonnie's question. "Appleton wasn't the kind to sit in his truck and watch us break into his house. I think he was already dead and his killer came back for evidence that would connect him to the murder."

"Someone else was in his truck?" Bonnie started to light another cigarette, then paused with the lighter inches from her face. "Do you think they're connected?"

"Who, Bon? Appleton and his killer?"

Fred decided to go after the ducks before Bonnie could answer.

"The murders, silly. Do you think the same guy killed Shelia?"

Bonnie waited for an answer while I watched Fred swim slowly toward the ducks. Goldens are great swimmers, but have nothing on Mallards. They let him get close then took off quacking, only to land a few yards away, and draw him further out in the lake.

"As sure as Fred will never catch those ducks," I said.

Bonnie turned toward Fred and laughed. He lunged at a duck but missed when they took flight again, leaving him with a mouth full of water. *Beethoven's Fifth* started playing on my cell phone before I could call Fred to come back. A quick glance at the text message told me it was the contractor who had replaced me with illegals.

"Looks like our sleuthing is on hold, Bon. I need to get my Jeep fixed. They want me to come back tomorrow and fix the mess made by the day laborers."

Fred should have been exhausted after his marathon swim trying to catch dinner, but the first thing he did when we got back to Bonnie's was jump out of her Cherokee and run after Chatter. I let him go after the tree-rat, and hiked up the path from Bonnie's to my cabin. Fred would be sleeping soundly tonight.

I spent the rest of the afternoon replacing the fuel pump on my old Jeep while Fred kept himself busy trying to catch the squirrel. The phone call to my new boss could wait.

Working on a car is one chore most people would rather pass on to a mechanic, but working on my old beast was different. I actually enjoyed it at times like this. It was better than alcohol or nicotine and a lot less work than jogging to get the endorphins flowing.

Unlike newer vehicles, with electric fuel pumps buried in unreachable gas tanks, my Jeep had the old-style mechanical pump attached to the engine block. And it didn't take a contortionist to get to it. There was enough room under the hood for a small army of back-yard mechanics, or in my case, a man and his dog.

Fred had tired of chasing the elusive Chatter, and parked himself under the Jeep so he could watch and supervise. He barked when my ratchet slipped and I let out a few cuss words to ease the pain of scraped knuckles. I realized he wasn't there to check my work at all when I heard the distinctive sound of bells and cannons; Beethoven was calling me.

The symphony stopped by the time I extracted myself from under the Jeep and stumbled up my front porch stairs to answer my phone. There was a message from Bonnie inviting me and Fred to dinner, and a text from the contractor wondering where I was. I sent a text back to the contractor explaining my Jeep was down and I wouldn't be there until tomorrow. Then I called Bonnie.

"Jake, you won't believe who called me," she said before I had a chance to speak. I was more surprised she knew it was me on the line than I was by the excitement in her voice; she didn't have caller ID.

"Alex Trebek?"

"No, silly. Why would *he* call me? It was Paula Morgan."

"The reporter?"

"Yes. I'm so excited, I could pee my pants. She wants to interview me on television."

"Be careful what you say, Bon. The police can use it against you."

"That's just it, Jake. Appleton left a suicide note in his truck. He confessed to killing Shelia."

Bonnie was so wound up, I didn't get many details. Our conversation went on for several more minutes without me learning much. However, she did invite me to dinner again; Patty had dropped by to celebrate with more food than they could possibly eat, and they wanted me to join them. Fred would be disappointed, but I begged off. I knew in my heart Appleton didn't kill himself or Shelia, and my heart also knew I wouldn't rest until I found the real killer. Not because of some altruistic sense of justice, but because whoever killed Appleton must have the two things that mean the most to me: Julie's wedding ring, and the copy of *Tom Sawyer* she gave me.

Those thoughts no sooner crossed my mind when Fred came up to lie by my feet. "Make that *three* things, Freddie. How could I forget you?"

CHAPTER SIX

I missed Bonnie's fifteen minutes of fame and our morning coffee the next two days. The job in Bailey demanded we get there early before the boss decided to replace me again. Bonnie met Paula Morgan at Three Sister's Park Thursday, so they could film where Appleton killed himself and left the suicide note exonerating Bonnie.

It wasn't until I got home, tired and dirty, that I was able to pick up my cell messages. Bonnie got a lot less than her fifteen minutes because Paula did most of the talking. She also wanted Fred and me to join her and watch the television interview. I didn't feel like talking to anyone. The physical labor had me exhausted, and all I wanted was a shower and some sleep. I would have sent her a text saying so, but I knew that would be rude. Bonnie doesn't text.

"Can't you record it, Bon," I asked after making the obligatory call and begging off. "We're so tired, well, at least I am. Fred slept most of the day when he wasn't hunting varmints."

She laughed. "You say the funniest things, Jake. Yes, I'll record it. Now you get some sleep."

By Friday afternoon, the job was finished, and once more I had some cash in my pocket. I thought I would stop off in Evergreen and get the pineapple pizza Bonnie liked so much, but got sidetracked when I noticed my Jeep was low on gas and stopped at the convenience store in Pine Junction. A fancy Mercedes SUV was pulling out as I pulled in. The car's windows were too darkly tinted to see the driver, but I immediately thought of Bonnie's mysterious SUV, the one that had driven by Appleton's cabin last Wednesday.

The temptation to drive past Appleton's cabin had been with me all week, so after buying a soda and lotto ticket, I gave the clerk twenty dollars and decided I'd drive by the cabin after pumping my gas.

Sometimes a person has to break the law, I told myself as I turned around to take the road to Appleton's. Sure, I could file a report with the Park County Sheriff, and hope I would get Julie's ring and book returned. I could have also just bought a winning lotto ticket. The odds of either were about the same. Of course, I had no guarantee I would find them in his cabin. After all, Bonnie and I had tried once with no success, so why did I think I would do any better this time?

Fred barked and woke me from my inner debate when we approached the cabin. Parked in the driveway was the Mercedes I had seen leaving the convenience store. Bonnie was right about it being expensive; people paid dearly for that circle with a three-pointed star I had saw as we drove by.

I was tempted to floor the Jeep and get away before we were spotted. Fortunately, I kept my cool, and neither sped up nor slowed down. Once I reached the bend in the road, I turned around and pulled over. My heart was beating faster than a hummingbird's wings. I couldn't approach the cabin now, but I needed to know who was inside, and what was he doing in there. Instinct said to wait until whoever it was left the cabin; then I could either go in or follow the Mercedes. My second option seemed the safest choice, for it didn't involve breaking any laws. I'm not a superstitious man, but it *was* Friday the thirteenth after all. Besides, I could always come back, but would probably never get another chance to find out who owned the expensive SUV.

We didn't have long to wait. I no sooner had my phone out to call Bonnie when I remembered it didn't work up here. Then Fred barked. I looked up from my phone in time to see the SUV race down the road toward 285. I managed to get a picture with my phone before starting my Jeep to give pursuit. Only the Jeep didn't start. "What the," I said, and then bit my tongue. I'm sure if Fred could talk, he would have finished for me because now he was barking non-stop.

"Hush, Fred. I need to hear the engine turn over." He quit barking, and I tried again. The distinctive click of the solenoid told me it was the battery. There wasn't enough juice to engage the starter.

Fred jumped out when I opened my door to check under the hood. "Stay!" I told him. "Don't you even think about chasing after that car." He actually obeyed, and got back into the Jeep. I'm sure if he thought there was any chance of catching the SUV, he would have ignored me.

The problem was simply a corroded battery cable. Luckily, my soda hadn't spilled in all the excitement, so I poured some on the corrosion that resembled green mold. The reaction reminded me of my boyhood days when I'd add baking soda to vinegar. After the fizzing died down, I wiped everything clean and tried starting the Jeep again. I'd like to say it purred like a kitten, but it really sounded more like a tomcat courting a female in heat.

It was time to put Plan A in motion and go commit another felony, but before I could get back out to close the hood, a sheriff's truck came down the road and stopped at my Jeep.

The deputy lowered his window. "Need a tow, sir?"

"Thanks, Officer," I said, and slammed the hood closed. "Just a loose cable, but I appreciate the offer."

He shut off his truck and picked up a microphone before I could get back in my Jeep. I froze. Could I be arrested for *thinking* about breaking and entering? "Negative on that ten-thirty-seven," he said.

I had no idea what a ten-thirty-seven was and didn't want to find out. "Well, take care of that beautiful dog," he said, before closing his window and driving off.

Plan A went south along with Plan B. I couldn't get away from Appleton's fast enough.

"This is really good," Bonnie said between bites of pizza. At least that's what I thought she said. Her mandibles were still working on the thick crust as she tried to talk.

"Glad you like it, but are you sure you wouldn't prefer a little dirt and gravel with it?"

She laughed then poured more honey on the crust.

The three of us were sitting at her kitchen table eating the pizza I finally got around to after the little side trip to Appleton's cabin. Half the pizza was gone by the time I had told her about our adventure and the run-in with the Sherriff's deputy who saved me and Fred from breaking into Appleton's cabin.

"So what do you think, Bon? Is it the same SUV you saw?"

She seemed to be deciding on whether to answer my question or take another bite of the pizza crust. "I can't tell from that picture, Jake. It's too small, but I can tell you what a ten-thirty-seven is. Wait here while I get my scanner codes." who saved me and Fred from breaking into Appleton's cabin.

I knew she kept the codes by her scanner, and wasn't surprised when she came back in less than a minute. Fred hardly had time to eat the crust of my pizza.

"Here it is," she said, positioning her glasses on her nose and holding the paper at arm's length. "Ten-thirty-seven, investigating suspicious vehicle. Someone must have reported you casing the joint."

"I wasn't there long enough. It must have been the SUV they reported, and the cop assumed it was me."

Bonnie put the scanner codes on the table and helped herself to another slice of pizza. "That explains why he didn't report us," she said.

"You mean when he drove by while we were trying to erase our fingerprints?"

"Of course, silly. What did you think I meant?"

She didn't wait for my answer, and went on talking. "He must have been waiting for us to leave, so he could break in."

"Which also means he doesn't live around there, or the neighbors wouldn't have called in a suspicious vehicle," I said, before being interrupted by Fred's 'feed me bark'. I tore off a piece of crust and threw it to him.

Bonnie looked a little hurt as she watched Fred devour his treat. "That's the best part, Jake."

She didn't have to explain. Julie had loved the crust too. It's why I always ordered thick-crust pizzas, for though I only cared for the center, Julie loved the taste of honey-coated pizza crust. "Sorry, Bon. I should have asked you first."

"Not for me, silly. You're missing the best part, and besides, that much people food can't be good for him."

I turned back to Fred who was watching my pizza like it was a cat. "What do you think, boy? Would you rather have dog food?"

He answered with another short bark, but this time I didn't feed him. "Speaking of people food, does Patty drive a Mercedes?"

Bonnie stared at me blankly.

"The food she brought you Wednesday night to celebrate not being a suspect anymore," I said, trying to explain how Patty had popped into my mind. "How well do you know her?"

A smile replaced the blank expression making her wrinkles less visible. "Like my own sister. I met her when I was going to CU and now I see her every Sunday at church. Why do you ask?"

"Watching Fred devour that pizza reminded me of turning down her home cooking. How come she knows so much about Mark Twain?"

"She worked at her daddy's bookstore in Boulder for years. He specialized in old and rare books so I guess she picked it up from him. That's where we first met. I would spend a lot of time browsing the old books after classes. Something you can't do much now that eBooks have put most of those stores out of business."

"Sorry, Bon, but if not for those eBooks, Fred and I would be eating squirrel."

Bonnie smiled at my remark then went back to her story. She had the faraway look in her eyes I used to see in my parents when they talked about the good old days. "She inherited the store when her father passed but had to close it several years ago. Surely you don't think she had anything to do with all this?"

"No, of course not. It was that thing about her telling Shelia she had one of the pirate copies. I guess she must have seen a chance to sell one of her father's old books. I'm really grasping at straws, Bon. I'm pretty sure Craig Renfield had something to do with Shelia's demise and probably killed Appleton too."

Bonnie looked horrified. "Are you saying Appleton didn't kill Shelia? I thought you gave up on that theory when he confessed. I hope you don't tell anyone else that. I'll be their prime suspect again."

"Mum's the word, Bon. Unless Fred tells someone, this won't leave the room; not that the cops would take me seriously."

She seemed to consider what I'd said for a moment before speaking again. "But some smart cop might come to the same conclusion. What if they do one of those tests on the suicide note like you see on TV all the time? If you're right, and someone forged the note after killing Appleton, they'll be back to looking for who really killed Shelia."

"I assume you're referring to a handwriting analysis. They don't have a reason to think otherwise, so I doubt they would bother. But we know better. There's no way he killed himself, and whoever killed Appleton wasn't working alone."

She didn't have to ask what I meant, her blank stare said it for her. The conversation had obviously taken a turn in the wrong direction. I could see she was getting upset. It was time to leave.

"The blood on his deck, Bon," I said, before wiping my mouth with a napkin, and standing. "I think Appleton was killed at his cabin then taken to Three Sisters where the murderer forged a suicide note."

Fred had been waiting patiently for more table scraps and must have sensed I was leaving. He left my side of the table and went over to beg from Bonnie.

Bonnie unconsciously fed him some of her crust before closing the pizza box. "And why do you think he had an accomplice?" she asked.

"Someone had to give the murderer a ride after parking Appleton's truck at the park," I said, waiting for Fred to join me.

She finally seemed to follow my reasoning. "So Craig killed Appleton at his cabin, then drove his truck to Three Sisters, wrote the note, and was picked up by someone. Have you figured out who that was, too?"

Fred didn't move from the table, where he watched Bonnie and the pizza.

"No, and I really don't care unless they have Julie's book and ring. I have no intention of bringing Appleton's killer to justice; that's a job for the police. All I want is to get Julie's property back. In the meantime, I've got to get back to the how-to book I've been writing, unless you have a better idea."

She silently handed me the pizza box. "What about the treasure? I'm sure if you put that great mind of yours on it, you could decode that riddle without even thinking about it."

I smiled at her unwitting contradiction. "I *have* thought about it, and came to the conclusion it's a hoax so Paul Wilson can sell more books. There is no lost gold, Bon."

Bonnie looked at me smugly, the way a child does when arguing with a parent. "Not according to Patty. She said she knew about it long before Wilson found the newspaper article. She remembers her father telling stories about how it was a big thing back in the twenties. Wilson didn't make that up."

Fred and I finished off the pizza somewhere around two in the morning. I couldn't concentrate on my chapter dealing with the importance of proper attic ventilation, so we had a cold snack before returning to my computer. I'd convinced myself that Julie would understand if she was watching. It was only one slice.

Bonnie's remark about Patty kept getting in the way, or maybe it was the thought of how much two hundred pounds of gold would be worth in today's market. If Appleton had decoded the original code, then what did the decoded message mean?

The words 'Blood sucking bug pass' were staring at me from Appleton's notebook paper. My how-to book had given way to finding the message and spending the last hour trying to solve the riddle. I even went so far as searching the *Rocky Mountain News* archives to find a copy of the original article, but got sidetracked about an article on a preacher who had crossed Mosquito Pass in snowshoes during the winter.

Father Dyer had become a legend for preaching to the mostly deaf ears of miners about the sins of gambling, drinking, and prostitution. My interest piqued when I read an article where he nearly died from a trip over Mosquito Pass in the winter when his feet froze during a bitter-cold snowstorm.

That's when it hit me. Pass referred to a mountain pass. If Drake was on his way to Leadville it had to be Mosquito Pass, a bloodsucking bug pass.

My first thought was to call Bonnie back and brag about unraveling the enigma. Then I had a flash image of someone listening to our phone messages. Now I knew how treasure hunting could lead to paranoia, and chided myself for being bit by gold fever. I decided to tell her tomorrow during coffee instead of calling, just to play it safe in case the NSA was listening.

CHAPTER SEVEN

Fred saved Bonnie from having to clean her kitchen floor when he ate the scrambled eggs she'd dropped after I told her about discovering the location of Drake's gold. "What are we waiting for, Jake? We need to get up there before someone else does!"

I should have waited until after breakfast before telling her. She didn't seem to notice the plate was empty when she set it in front of me. "What's this, we? Margot would have my scalp if I ever took you to the top of that pass. Do you have any idea what the lack of oxygen at that altitude can do to a chain smoker?"

She looked over at a pack of cigarettes on the table then picked it up. "I can go without you, you know," she said while tapping the pack to make a filter tip appear.

Not wanting another argument like we had the other day when she had insisted on going to Appleton's cabin, I tried to change the subject. "Not on an empty stomach, Bon. Besides, I think I should verify the code from another copy of *Tom Sawyer* before going off half-cocked," I said, pointing to my plate.

She took one look at my plate and then looked down at Fred, who was patiently sitting at her side waiting for more eggs. "What's there to verify?" she asked, patting him on the head and smiling. "What else can blood sucking pass mean? Any school kid can see that. If we don't get our butts up there right away, someone else is going to beat us to the treasure."

I got up from the table with my empty plate and went over to the counter by her range. "We're the only ones besides Appleton who knows the deciphered code, and I doubt if he's going up there anytime soon." I knew the only way I was going to get breakfast was to make it myself, so I started cracking more eggs into Bonnie's mixing bowl.

"How can you be so sure?"

"Because he's dead, Bon."

"Not, Appleton! Jeeze, Louise, don't be so dense. How can you be so sure someone else hasn't decoded the message already? That author, what's his name, didn't strike me as no dummy, and then there's those punk kids."

"Paul Wilson. I suppose it's possible now that you mention it. He must have known about Father Dyer. Good thing he didn't have the key, or I'm sure he would have figured it out by now. But I don't see how those kids could solve a Ranger Rick crossword puzzle, let alone decode Drake's message."

"The key? Oh I get it, the right book is the key."

I picked out another egg and cracked it on the side of the bowl. "Do you want two or three?"

Bonnie quit playing with her cigarettes and came over to the range. "Just two, and get yourself more coffee while I cook these. Then we're going up there together, whether you like it or not."

"Okay, Bon, you win. But we take my Jeep this time." I knew if I didn't give in, she would go without me.

We were lost, and my Jeep was hissing at us for lack of water by the time we made it to Fairplay.

"Stay on highway two eighty-five for point five more miles, then turn right on highway nine and proceed toward Breckinridge." Lucy, the name Julie had given my GPS because it was always sending us in the wrong direction, was trying to make herself heard over the knocking of the engine. Julie had said the GPS reminded her of Lucille Ball in the old movie *The Long Long Trailer* because that Lucy was always sending Ricky in the wrong direction, too.

I didn't have a clue where to find the pass between Fairplay and Leadville, but couldn't let on to Bonnie that I was lost, so I told Lucy what I thought of her directions and unplugged her to shut her up.

Bonnie interrupted my discourse with Lucy when she spotted an old-fashioned gas station. "They might have water, Jake, and I'm sure someone can tell you how to get to Mosquito Pass."

"I'm afraid those service stations went out with black-and-white TV," I said, but pulled in anyway. To my amazement, it did have a water spigot and air hose at the end of the island. I also noticed the pumps didn't take credit cards. I felt like we must have entered a time-warp.

Fred barked and started pacing back and forth on the rear seat.

"Do you mind taking him over there while I give the old Jeep a drink?" I asked, pointing to a patch of grass on the side of the station.

They weren't gone two minutes when a real, live attendant came out from the service bay after I had the hood open. I'd expected to see Goober from the *Andy Griffith Show*, but this guy was the complete opposite. He could have been Appleton's twin, except his tattoos were barely recognizable underneath the grease and oil on his arms.

"Be careful there, buddy," he said. "Better use my rag on that cap, so she don't scald you when you open it." He wiped his hands on the rag before offering it to me. I couldn't help notice it made his hands dirtier.

"Thanks, but it'll be okay once I let the pressure off," I said, turning the cap a quarter turn so it would release the pressure but not fly off.

He smiled and nodded his head when steam and water came rushing out the overflow tube onto the ground. "Well, looks like you know what you're doing so I'll get out of your hair. Let me know if you need anything else," he said before heading back to his service bay.

"We could use some directions to Mosquito Pass," Bonnie said. She had returned with Fred when my head was under the hood.

The attendant stopped in his tracks, and turned around. "If I could get a dollar for everyone who's asked that question, ma'am, I'd be a millionaire," he said as he walked back toward us.

"I should print me a map and start selling them. It'd be a great way to advertise my towing business. You wouldn't believe how many people try to make it over that pass without four-wheel drive. But you shouldn't have any problem with this old baby. You got one of the true four-wheel drives with that old Quadra-Trac. You could climb Mount Everest with that thing."

"Maybe Pike's Peak, once I get this radiator fixed," I said, pointing to a small leak, spitting more steam than water. "You wouldn't believe how hard it is to find anyone who repairs the old copper cores anymore."

He took a card from his pocket and handed it to me. "My name's Rick, I'd be happy to order you a new plastic core, but I don't suppose you'd want to wait for it."

"No, it's not that bad. Not yet."

"Well, call me from your cell if you run out of water up there. I'm the local tow service for Triple A and several others."

Bonnie saw her chance to cut in. "Cell phones work up there? Maybe you can get directions from that fancy phone of yours, Jake, seeing as you're too busy jawing to get directions."

Rick flashed several rotten teeth when he smiled at Bonnie's remark. "Yes, ma'am. We got several towers on the top of the mountain. Covers most of Leadville and even reaches Breckenridge. I expect to get a call from some kids who were here this morning anytime now. Darn fools were driving a Datsun pickup."

"Did they have tattoos and weird hair?" I asked, watching him take a pinch of tobacco from a can that seemed to appear from nowhere.

"How'd you know?"

"I saw one of those trucks just last week, driven by some kids who were at a book signing, and they didn't strike me as kids who read much. I remember it because my dad gave me a truck just like it on my sixteenth birthday," I said, removing the radiator cap and reaching for the water hose.

Rick turned his head and spit before wiping a greasy hand on his coveralls. "Ah, was afraid they was friends of yours." Then he turned toward Bonnie. "As for those directions, ma'am, just keep going north on nine and you'll see a road on the left, just before Alma, called Mosquito Gulch Road. If you get to Alma, you missed it, and gone too far."

He took another pinch of tobacco and put it under his tongue. "I gotta get back to the oil change I was working on, but look out for those fools. Don't like to see nobody get hurt up there."

"Sure, and thanks for your help," I said as I got into my Jeep. "That old Datsun won't be hard to miss."

Bonnie paused before letting Fred into the Jeep so she could wave bye to Rick. Then, almost immediately, she covered her mouth instead. Rick had chosen that particular moment to spit tobacco juice on the ground.

Rick's comment about the punk kids kept nagging at me on our ascent up Mosquito Gulch Road. Had they found a way to decipher the code, too? My thoughts were interrupted when we came to a fork in the road. "Did Rick say which way to turn?" I asked my new navigator. I'd turned Lucy off shortly after leaving the gas station.

Bonnie had recovered from the spitting incident, and was studying a road map she found in my glove box. "No, and this map is worthless. I can't even find the road we're on."

I pointed to a handmade sign for Leadville pointing to the right. "No problem, Ms. Yossarian. I asked too soon."

Bonnie looked up from the map she was trying to fold back together. "Don't think I don't know who you meant, Mr. Smarty Pants. I was teaching literature before you were born. *Catch 22* was one of my favorites."

My mind had already gone on to the road ahead and so I didn't answer her. What little research I had done on the trail before leaving home said not to attempt the road into Leadville. It was narrow, with switchbacks that clung to the side of the mountain. One slip and it was two thousand feet straight down. I had no plans on going that far, or Bonnie would indeed wet her pants if she should look out the window. But we were safe for now. The path was rocky and getting steeper, with mountains on both sides and no sign of any precipitous drop-offs, so I didn't mention the danger ahead.

After another two miles, the road forked left with another sign saying we had reached 11,500 feet, and from this point on it was four-wheel drive only. My old Jeep must not have liked the altitude, because it began to overheat again, letting out a cloud of steam from under the hood.

"My God, Jake, are we on fire!" Bonnie had her hand on the door latch and was ready to make a quick exit.

"Just a little steam, Bon."

Fred barked his two cents from the back seat, so I stopped the Jeep before I had a mutiny.

"Okay, everyone out. Let's look around while old Betsy cools off."

Unlike when we stopped earlier, this time the engine was really hot. I knew better than to pour what little water I carried into a boiling radiator; not only would it be a waste of water, but the possibility of cracking an engine block or head was too great.

Bonnie must have been confident the Jeep wasn't on fire, and poked her head under the open hood. "We won't get stuck up here, I hope."

"No, but we should turn back after it cools down. It gets really cold once the sun goes down at this altitude."

"But we just got here, Jake. Can't you do something to get it going sooner?"

Fred had been sitting, watching, and listening to us talk. Then, for no apparent reason, he barked, and ran to a nearby snowdrift. Summer snow storms and drifts were not uncommon at this elevation. It made me check the sky. The last thing I needed was to be caught in a thunderstorm. Lightning kills more people in the high country than avalanches do in the winter.

"I don't have to, Bon. Fred just found a way to cool off the radiator for us."

She gave me her blank look again.

"The snow, Bon. We can use it to cool the radiator."

"Won't that crack the block or something?"

"I won't put it on the engine, just the radiator. If we cool the radiator off, it should help cool off the engine faster."

Fred was already rolling in the snow before I got there, and came running back to me with a mouth full of it when he saw me. I don't think he had read my mind about putting snow on the radiator, so I guessed he wanted to play. I reached down to thank him with a pat on the head and realized the snow was red.

"Did Fred cut himself?" Bonnie asked when she caught up with us.

I knew it wasn't blood from its oily feel. "No, someone has a transmission leak."

"And how could you possibly know that, Sherlock?"

"Engine oil would be black; this came from an automatic. It looks like they were parked here for a while before turning back."

Bonnie went over to where Fred had been, reached down to check for herself, then looked up at me like I'd just answered a million dollar question on a quiz show. "How do you know that stuff? And what makes you think they didn't go on to Leadville?"

"Look at the trail of transmission fluid going back toward Fairplay. The spots get smaller and further apart before disappearing altogether."

She held her hand flat across her brow. It must have been more out of habit than necessity for the sun was already behind her. "So, what does that prove?"

"If they continued on to Leadville, there would be fluid going that way too."

She considered my logic for a moment then changed the subject. "Do you think it was those kids?"

"Not unless someone put an automatic from a Nissan in their truck. I don't think the early Datsuns came with anything but a stick. Mine had a four speed which was a pain in the butt for a kid learning to drive."

Fred dropped his mouthful of snow at my feet and barked. It was a game we played in the winter, so I scooped it up and made a snowball. He knew how far I'd throw it and was already headed for the spot when I let it sail. It gave me time to fill my baseball cap with a load of the white stuff and head back toward the Jeep. Bonnie followed with her headscarf full of snow, looking like a bag lady that had run out of shopping bags.

I didn't see the footprints leading away from the road until my second trip back to the snowdrift.

CHAPTER EIGHT

The angle of the setting sun created shadows I hadn't seen earlier. There were half a dozen footprints in the snow leading north toward the closest hillside. There might have been more, but several vehicles had been through here after the prints were left. I saw deep tire tracks from a heavy truck, and several narrower ones that could only be a motorcycle or ATV. A lot of people used this trail for off-road fun, which explained why most of the footprints had been obliterated. I also knew there had been more than one person because one of the prints was much smaller than the others. Bonnie and Fred watched as I got on my hands and knees to get a closer look.

Fred came over to see what was so interesting. "How about it, boy, think you can find where those footprints go to?" I suspected he thought I'd found something good to eat, but was willing to give him credit for wanting to help.

"Do you think it was those kids?" Bonnie didn't bother to bend down to our level.

"Maybe, but I can't help wonder what they were doing over there," I answered pointing to where the prints led.

Bonnie's eyes followed the path in the snow. "Well whoever it is, I don't give a rat's ass anymore. I'm cold and getting scared we might get stuck up here in that old Jeep of yours. Can we come back and look some other time?" She had dressed in shorts and a thin summer blouse. Great attire for the near eighty temps back in Denver, but nothing a Sherpa would be caught wearing at this altitude.

"My thoughts exactly. And the sooner we head home, the better. Unless they were leaving breadcrumbs from a jelly donut, Fred would never find their scent anyway."

Bonnie and Fred both slept on the way home, which was fine with me. It gave me nearly two hours of quiet solitude to think about how foolish we had been thinking we could simply drive up to Mosquito Pass and find the treasure. We had barely started up the trail and must have seen the remnants of at least two dozen mines. There were probably over a hundred more in the area and any one of them could have been where Drake had hidden his treasure, if there was one. Even Wilson said his book was a work of fiction based on an old news article.

Thinking of Paul Wilson reminded me of the punk kids. What were they doing up there? Had they solved Drake's riddle within a riddle? The owner of the gas station had said they were only a few hours ahead of us, so unless they went on to Leadville, we should have passed them on our way up Mosquito Gulch as they were coming back. Then again, they could have gone north on Colorado Nine to Breckenridge before we'd made the turn toward the pass. I hoped that was the case, for the road into Leadville was a widow maker in a two-wheel-drive Datsun pickup.

Mosquito Pass still bugged me as I sat at my computer Sunday morning working on my how-to eBook. My mind kept drifting while staring at the nearly blank computer screen. I had the title for the chapter, How to Stop Dry Rot Dead, and that was all I had written. I finally shut down the computer and called Fred. Maybe some great revelation would come to me during our walk around the lake.

Like our morning walk, the revelation on dry rot would have to wait. A county Mountie was in my driveway checking out my Jeep. Trouble is, he was checking in the wrong county. His truck said Park County Sheriff and I live in Jefferson County.

"Stay, Fred," I said, opening the door. Maybe I should have used reverse psychology and said go. He obeyed as well as a teenager and was the first one out the door.

The deputy stopped writing in his notebook long enough to reach down and pat Fred on the head before addressing me. "Is this your Jeep, sir?"

"What I do, Officer? Get caught by a red-light camera or something?"

"Then you must be Jacob Martin," he said extending his hand. "I'm Officer White from the Park County Sheriff's Department. I'd like to ask you a few questions about your trip yesterday."

Fred tired of the chit-chat and went in search of a bush. I invited the officer inside my house once I realized he wasn't here to arrest me for breaking and entering Appleton's cabin.

White took in everything the second he stepped through the entrance of my small cabin, including the dirty dishes stacked in my kitchen sink. Even my bedroom door was open, exposing an unmade bed. My bathroom was the only room he couldn't see because that door was closed. He must have been disappointed if he'd been expecting a meth lab, or stacks of stolen electronics.

I offered him a chair at my kitchen table, facing away from the clutter in the sink and on the counter. "I've got a half a pot of coffee from breakfast this morning. I can warm it in the microwave if you care for a cup."

"No thank you, Jacob. Or do you go by Jake?"

"Everyone, except my ex, calls me Jake. I won't repeat what she calls me." I no sooner let it out my mouth when I realized how dumb the cliché sounded. I chalked it up to nerves.

"I'm sorry to bother you, Jake, but we need to follow up all possible leads in a case like this. My brother-in-law owns a service station in Fairplay, and claims a man and older woman with a Golden, like the one that greeted me, stopped at his place yesterday asking questions about a couple kids. My captain was wondering if you saw them on your trip up to Mosquito Pass."

His brother-in-law? It made me wonder if his captain was some relation too. I thought I'd left nepotism back in the Ozarks. "We didn't get very far. My Jeep overheated and by the time it cooled off it was too late to go any further. But I can tell you we never saw the kids, or anyone else. Why do you ask? Did they rob a bank or something?"

He missed my futile attempt at humor, and hesitated before answering. It was obvious he was considering his words carefully. "They've been reported missing."

I got up from the table when I heard the microwave beep. I had put a cup in for myself even if he didn't want one. "Sure I can't warm you up a cup, Officer?"

"Bob. You can call me Bob, no need to be formal. I only want to ask a few questions."

I almost laughed when he said his name was Bob, but caught myself in time.

Officer White saw through me. "I know, Jake. I've heard more jokes about bobwhites than I can count. My parents had a cruel sense of humor."

Fred scratched at the door, so I went over to let him in before I made a total fool of myself. "Oh, we did find this," I said reaching down to rub my hand on Fred's back. I was too tired to give Fred a bath after our failed treasure hunt and was hoping his swim in the lake would clean off the oil. Now I was glad I hadn't destroyed what might be evidence.

White looked at my oily hand without touching it. "I'm afraid I don't understand."

"Transmission fluid. We stopped by a snowdrift and when my dog rolled in the snow, he came up with this. Someone with a leaky transmission had parked at the same spot before us. But I don't think it was the kids."

White stopped writing and looked up at me. His expression screamed "What?" without saying a word. I felt compelled to explain. "I don't think the truck they were driving had an automatic, so they couldn't be the people who hiked to a nearby mine."

"Someone parked a vehicle and then hiked over to a mine? I thought you said you hadn't seen anyone?"

Bonnie walked in before I could answer. "You all right, Jake?" She was as white as one of my printer papers, and her face was just as blank.

I tried to ease the situation by joking. "Officer White, this is Bonnie, my partner in crime." Dracula couldn't have done a better job in draining what little blood that was left in her face.

White rose from his chair, and walked over to shake her hand. "Ah, the third member of the Three Musketeers. Glad to meet you, ma'am. Jake was just telling me about the trip the three of you took yesterday."

She accepted his hand cautiously, as though she was afraid he'd snap handcuffs on her. "I thought Jake might be in trouble or something when I saw your truck drive by. He had a burglary a couple days ago so one can't be too careful."

White turned back toward me. "Burglary?"

"Yeah, someone broke down my lower door and stole a bunch of stuff. I reported it to the Jefferson County sheriff, but they never found the guy."

"He even told them who it was, and they did nothing," Bonnie said.

White wrote a couple more notes in his book while answering Bonnie. "I'm sure they haven't forgotten. Jeffco has a huge area to cover and a lot more crime. The most exciting thing we've had lately is a break-in after the owner of the house committed suicide."

Her jaw literally dropped. I always thought the expression was nothing more than an idiom for unimaginative writers, but she was on the verge of losing her dentures. I jumped in before she could confess. "I think I heard about that. Wasn't it over by Bailey?"

"Not even close. He lived right over the county line in Pine Junction," Bob answered before Bonnie could pass out. "But tell me about the hikers you didn't see. The ones you think had a leaky transmission, and why you don't think they're our missing persons." He was like a bulldog --or is that an elephant?-- he hadn't forgotten about my hypothesis.

"Those Datsuns didn't have automatics," Bonnie answered for me. Evidently she had recovered from the thought of spending the night in jail.

"Datsuns?" White asked.

It was my turn to interrupt. "Your brother-in-law, Rick, told us the kids were driving a Datsun."

"And Jake used to have one of them, so he figured out all by himself it wasn't the kids." Bonnie finished for me.

White looked like he was getting upset. "Okay, maybe I will have that cup of coffee after all, and then we'll start over but I only need one of you to tell me the story."

"Do you mind Bon? You make better coffee than me anyway," I said while leading Officer White back to my kitchen table.

Bonnie busied herself with making fresh coffee and cleaning my dirty dishes while I explained how Fred had found the transmission fluid and tracks leading to the mine. I also added my two cents about why the footprints couldn't belong to the kids with a brief history of early Datsun pickup trucks. But for the life of me, I couldn't think of a way to ask about Appleton without incriminating myself or Bonnie. I suppose Fred was just as guilty, but I didn't think they'd arrest him.

"Do you think they're on to us, Jake?" Bonnie asked while lighting a cigarette. The three of us were sitting on my front porch watching White drive away.

I didn't bother acting annoyed over the smoke, for I knew she needed the nicotine to calm her nerves. "Not yet. I was surprised Bobwhite didn't say something about my Jeep breaking down by Appleton's. Unless that deputy never called in my plates, they must have a record of me being in the vicinity of the break in."

"Bobwhite? Why did you call him that?"

"It's his name," I answered with a short laugh. "Officer Robert White, or as he prefers to be called, Bob."

The irony of his name made her smile, but only for a moment.

"I only hope the burglary was discovered before the other deputy saw me there. Then there would be no reason to suspect me, unless the CBI finds some prints we missed when we tried to wipe the place down."

"CBI?"

"Colorado's version of the FBI. I doubt that Park County can afford a modern forensics lab, so I assume they outsource it to the state."

Bonnie tapped cigarette ashes into her hand, and seemed to be considering my explanation. "What about the blood on the deck, Jake? What if the CBI finds it *and* our prints? Won't they think we killed him?"

Fred had been sitting and listening to every word, so I tried to lighten things up a bit. "What do you think about Mexico, Freddie? Would you like to meet a cute Chihuahua?"

Bonnie wasn't amused. "Seriously, Jake. How can you joke at a time like this? I nearly died when they thought I killed Shelia. Now I'm a suspect again!"

"I'm sorry, Bon. Even if they do connect me as the one who wiped the place clean, they have nothing on you. I promise I won't say a word about you being there."

Her eyes began to swell with tears, and she spoke without looking at me. "I'm sorry I was so self-centered, Jake. You remind me so much of my Diane. She didn't have a selfish bone in her body either."

Fred and I finally made it to the lake after Bonnie recovered and went home for something stronger than coffee. By the looks of the overflowing parking lot, it wasn't going to be easy finding a place away from the weekend crowd where he could swim. And to make matters worse, someone had posted a new sign with a list of don'ts. Halfway down the list, right after 'no power boats' was 'no swimming'. It looked like civilization was finally catching up with me.

I kept Fred on his leash until we were once again on the backside of the lake. 'Dogs must be on a leash' was also on the list, but I knew it was more for the parks protection from lawsuits than anything else, for half the dogs there were Labs or Goldens, running free or swimming. Now all I had to do was trick Fred into a bath by pretending to play fetch with a stick. Maybe I'd forget about our little adventure from the day before once his oily fur was clean again. I had better things to think about than the lost kids who were probably in Vegas or somewhere far away by now.

I'd convinced myself they either made it down the trail to Leadville or had gone on to Breckenridge. Deputy White had said that none of the search teams found a trace of their Datsun, so I concluded they had probably run away, and left the state by now. I had to concentrate on finding Appleton's killer before the CBI found Fred's prints and came after me. Now I wished I'd taken the time to clean his tracks in the kitchen.

A young couple stopped to watch Fred swim after the stick I had been throwing for him. They reminded me of Craig and Shelia the last time I saw them together. Unlike Craig, this guy didn't seem bothered by Fred being loose. He and his girlfriend were laughing and holding hands when Fred jumped in the water.

Thinking of Craig brought me back to the murders. I was sure he had killed Shelia and Appleton, but how could I prove it? I would look really foolish if I called Deputy White and told him that he should arrest Craig Renfield. Without motive and some proof that he did it, White would have me locked up, not for murder but for insanity.

The more I thought about it, the more I realized I was grasping at straws. But who else could have killed Appleton, and why? That's when I realized I'd been playing detective all wrong. I needed to start with the *why* instead of the *who*.

Appleton stole my copy of *Tom Sawyer* so he could decode Drake's enigma. It only followed that whoever killed him knew he had found the answer to the riddle. Bingo. That was why the punk kids were on the pass; they hadn't solved the riddle, they took the answer from Appleton. Damn, I really wanted to see Renfield hang, and it wasn't going to happen. Now I had the why and the who, but I still had no proof it was the kids.

My brilliant deductive reasoning ended when Fred dropped a stick at my feet. At least I thought it had been brilliant, though I'm sure Deputy White would compare it to a night-light — dim and dull. I threw the stick back in the water then headed toward the parking lot. It wasn't two minutes later I felt Fred trying to put the stick in my hand.

"No, Fred!" I said a little too loud. "We need to get on home and do some research on those kids. I don't even know their names."

He had a limited vocabulary, so I doubt he understood what I'd said, but he did know the word NO, and dropped the stick.

Fred was still pouting when we got home. I wasn't sure if it was because he thought I'd yelled at him, or he was mad that I'd cut his swim too short. Whatever it was, he wanted to let me know he didn't like it. I ignored him and let him stay outside to sulk while I went in to boot my computer.

It didn't take long to get the names of the punk kids. A search with the keywords 'missing' and 'Park County' returned an article on the search underway on Mosquito Pass for a Jennifer Dawson and Cory Weston of Lakewood. Another search, this time using 'Cory Weston' and 'Lakewood, Colorado', gave me an address on Saulsbury. I quickly checked my notes for Craig's address. They lived on the same block.

I couldn't wait to share my knowledge with someone and gave Bonnie a call.

When she didn't pick up, I called her cell phone. "Did you hear the news, Jake?" she asked before I could tell her about my fortuitous research. "They found those kids in a mine on Mosquito Pass."

"Are they okay?"

"No. They're—"

My phone beeped and cut her off momentarily. "Hold on, Bon. It's the Park County Sheriff calling. I better get it."

CHAPTER NINE

"Don't say a word to them until you talk to a lawyer, Bonnie. I'll ask Harvey first thing tomorrow and see if he can help you." Bonnie's twin sister, Margot, didn't let me finish talking before adding her two-cents. I had just finished telling them about my conversation with Deputy White and how he wanted us to sign a written statement. Bonnie and Margot were at a boutique in Evergreen when her call had been interrupted by the Sheriff's office. When I called back, Margot insisted I come down and tell them everything White had said. After I'd told her I wouldn't be caught dead in a boutique, we agreed to meet at the coffee shop two doors down.

I knew better than to interrupt Margot by suggesting a lawyer wasn't necessary, especially one like Harvey Goldstein, Denver's finest. Margot was a major pain in my neck last year when she and Bonnie had talked me into re-writing a manuscript their father had written. Little did I know it would lead to a trail of deceit and murder and get me accused of negligent homicide. I hadn't seen Margot since then, and it still amazed me how alike, yet different, two twins could be. I suppose it was the money.

Margot had married well and didn't mind spending on anything that would make her look younger. Bonnie's dead husband left her with a mortgaged house and a Social Security check that barely paid the utilities and grocery bill. She couldn't afford the expensive facials, and beauty treatments her sister could. Margot looked twenty years younger, from a distance. Sitting next to her in the coffee shop with her makeup, Botox, and tired face lift, she looked like a clown.

Bonnie winced after sipping her latte. "I can't afford a lawyer, Margot. You know that. And don't even suggest paying for one. I don't need your charity."

Other than being too sweet for my taste, I knew there was nothing wrong with her coffee that a little bourbon wouldn't fix. I tried to stop the argument that was sure to follow. "Whoa, you two. White only wants a statement. He just called to let me know they found the bodies and thank me for telling him about the transmission fluid. He said they would have missed it otherwise."

Margot looked at me with swollen eyelids. "Transmission fluid?"

I hesitated answering, wondering if she had been crying. Had they been arguing before I arrived? Then

I saw the scars and realized it must have been from her latest elective surgery.

Bonnie didn't wait for me to speak. "Jake told him it wasn't the kids because their truck didn't have an automatic. He got all that from a little spot of oil on the ground."

"Except I didn't take into account a power-steering pump," I said, cutting back into the conversation.

Both sisters sat their drinks down at the same time and looked at me, four gray-blue eyes wondering what I had just said.

"I'm pretty sure the early Datsuns didn't have power-steering, so it never occurred to me that it was the pump that was leaking. Someone must have added it. Anyway, those pumps use a fluid that looks exactly like transmission fluid."

Margot looked annoyed. She had fished out a compact from her purse to check her eyelids while I was talking. "That's nice, Jake, but what did the sheriff say about the kids?"

"I was getting to it, Margot. White said they found the Datsun in a pit half a mile from the mine. That's when they decided to check out all the mines in the area. The kids were in the one where we saw the footprints in the snow. The old rotten floor gave out on them, and they fell fifty feet straight down."

Margot didn't wait for me to continue and put away her compact. Evidently, she was satisfied with what she had seen in the mirror, or maybe it had cracked and she didn't want us to know. "All the more reason you need a lawyer, Bonnie. I won't be surprised if they say you two ditched the truck after throwing the kids down the mine shaft. I know these cops. They'll pretend you're their best friends and then slam it to you."

Bonnie's eyes turned a shade darker. "This isn't a television cop show, Margot. All they want is a statement. If I go in there with a lawyer, I might as well hang a scarlet M on my chest."

"I still think it's a trick. They'll find out you were in that guy's house sooner or later. You should let them know before they find out. That's why you need a lawyer."

"You told her we went into Appleton's cabin?" I asked, raising my voice.

Bonnie lowered her head, and stared into her latte. "She's my sister, Jake. I guess I let it slip."

I took a deep breath and cleared my throat to get their attention. "We don't even know if the burglary White mentioned was Appleton's. Nor do we know if they suspect murder. Are you forgetting they said Appleton killed himself? Why incriminate ourselves and make them think otherwise?"

"Because Bonnie will be charged for withholding evidence when they find out she was there. Ow! Why'd you kick me?"

"Because everyone's listening," Bonnie answered.

I hadn't seen Bonnie kick her sister under the table, but looked around to see that we had indeed become the coffee shop's main event. "Well, if you gals don't mind, Fred's been alone in the car too long, and I need to get going," I said, getting up and reaching for my wallet. It was a white-lie. I had left Fred home on my front deck, but it was all I could think of to make a quick exit.

"I'll get it, Jake," Margot said when I opened my empty wallet in front of her while trying to extract a credit card. "And I promise not to call Harvey — for now."

Fred ran out to greet me with a tennis ball in his mouth when I drove into my driveway twenty minutes later. I hope if there is such a thing as reincarnation that I come back as a Golden. They have a way of making one smile no matter what. I took the slimy ball and threw it down the hill, knowing it should give me time to make it to my porch before he came back to drop it at my feet.

Our game went on for over half an hour, long enough for me to plan my next move. I didn't want to pin my future on Margot's promise. I knew all too well she could have second thoughts and tell Harvey everything, thinking it would be best for Bonnie. If she did spill the beans or talk Bonnie into coming clean, I could forget about ever getting Julie's book and ring back. Once they suspected Appleton had been murdered, his loot would become evidence, assuming it was found, and I would become the number one suspect. In the end, I decided to hold off a few days before going to the Sheriff's substation in Bailey with Bonnie to give our statements. I wasn't ready to perjure myself in the event Margot got Bonnie to confess. I needed time to gather more information before making any decision that could put me in jail for several years.

Once Fred was fed and lying at my feet, I went to the one source of information that never failed me: the Internet. I had convinced myself that it was the kids who killed Appleton when he caught them in the act of a break-in, but now I wasn't so sure. My gut told me Appleton didn't kill himself, nor did the kids die in an accident. That left Mr. Jerk as my only suspect, so I decided to run the cheapskate's version of a background check on Renfield.

Craig Renfield turned out to be of the generation that had little to do with computers and social media. I couldn't find him on Facebook, YouTube, or LinkedIn. Next, I tried Cory and Jennifer.

Cory kept his Facebook page private. Jennifer, however, seemed to have nothing to hide. She discussed in full detail all the things she and Cory were going to buy with the money they would get from Drake's treasure. She also didn't mind sharing her personal thoughts through her poetry. There were crude attempts at writing sonnets with only twelve lines and no clue about iambic pentameter. But it didn't matter, for after reading several of them, I felt terrible for thinking this poor kid could have killed anyone.

It was obvious she had been abused as a child; abandoned by her father before she could walk and ignored by a drunken mother. Cory had saved her from taking her life only last year and the two of them were deeply in love. She moved in with him when she was only sixteen without any objection from her mother. Cory was her knight in shining armor, and the father of her unborn child.

I gave up searching when my Internet connection went dead around midnight. This happened whenever Bonnie would turn off the power strip to her router. She was close enough, so I didn't have to pay for service of my own, but at times like this I wish I wasn't so frugal.

The low-down on Renfield would have to wait, as would the solution to my problem of finding Julie's book and ring. Fred was already asleep at my feet, so I shut down my computer and quietly headed for the bedroom. Whoever said dogs could hear twice as good as humans must have had a Golden. He woke and followed me before I made it two feet.

Sleep failed to produce the answer to my problem. I still had no idea who killed whom when I woke Monday morning. Instead, my subconscious kept nagging me about a more pressing predicament — what to do about Margot and her lawyer. Seeing as how it was Bonnie's predicament too, Fred and I went knocking on her door. I'm sure his only concern was if he'd like what was for breakfast.

We could smell sausage frying even before we let ourselves in. Once inside, I went straight for the coffee pot. "This smells so good, Bon. It's just what I need to wake up. Poor Fred has no idea what he's missing." I loved her coffee. Unlike the generic store brands I always bought on sale, she insisted on nothing but Columbian beans picked by Juan Valdez himself.

She smiled and rubbed Fred's head. "Acid reflux, according to Doctor Oz." Then she looked up at me like a worried mother. "Don't tell me you were up all night at that computer again?"

"Not after your router went down. But in a way, I'm glad you shut me off last night. I probably would have fallen asleep at my desk again. That really hurts this old back."

"I'm sorry, Jake. I keep forgetting about that switch." Almost every room in her house had an outlet for a lamp controlled by a wall switch. That was the building code back in the seventies when ceiling lights were not in fashion. Her router was plugged into one of those outlets.

Fred decided he wanted out, which seemed strange considering the wonderful smells of breakfast cooking. But nature must take precedence over food in the animal kingdom, so I left the kitchen counter where I had been standing and opened the back door for him.

"Do you think Margot can keep her word?" I asked without looking at her so I could watch Fred to make sure he didn't stray too far.

When she didn't answer, I quit watching Fred and turned toward her. She looked really upset. "Bon? Are you okay?"

"You'll have to go without me, Jake. Margot insists I wait until her lawyer can go with me to make my statement. You know how she can be. Money does that to people. Makes them think they know best."

Fred interrupted our conversation by barking before I could tell her I had decided to wait a few days myself. I quickly turned, and looked outside to see what had him so upset. Someone was driving up the road to my cabin with Fred chasing after him.

I yanked the door open, and yelled out before running down her back steps, "My God, Bon! It's the SUV from Appleton's! Wait here and call 911 if you hear any gunshots!"

I was completely out of breath by the time I ran up the path to my house. It was less than fifty yards, but it was all uphill. Fred had the driver trapped in his car, afraid to get out. When I got closer, I noticed a man with a neatly trimmed goatee, a horseshoe ring of hair, and thick glasses sitting behind the wheel. He was the author from the book signing.

"Down, boy. It's okay," I said to Fred, grabbing him by his collar.

"Mr. Martin?" Paul Wilson opened his window halfway, but didn't make a move to get out of his car.

Bonnie's Cherokee raced into my driveway before I could respond. "I called the sheriff," she said through her open window. "They should be here..." She stopped short when she saw who it was.

Wilson finally found the nerve to leave his car and surprised me when he stood next to it. He barely made it to the top of its door. He had looked much taller at the signing, but then he might have been standing on some kind of platform at the time.

"I'm sorry to come unannounced, Mr. Martin, but I assure you I'm not here to hurt anyone."

"It's okay. She didn't really call the cops. Did you, Bon?"

She shook her head no.

"Please call me Jake," I said, extending my hand. "And the speechless lady is my good neighbor, Bonnie Jones. I think you already met my dog, Fred."

Wilson returned the handshake without looking at me. His eyes never left Fred. "Yes, I remember him from the bookstore. He didn't look so vicious then."

Bonnie found her voice and came over to hold Fred. "He's a pussycat most of the time. It's that car you're driving he doesn't like."

"My car?" Wilson asked. "What's he got against my car?"

"He saw one just like it at a crime scene a few days ago." She no longer seemed to be afraid of Wilson. Maybe it was because he was a good inch or two shorter than her.

He looked over at her Cherokee. "That was *your* Jeep?" he asked in a much stronger voice. "What were *you* doing there?" For some reason, the situation reminded me of the time when Fred had cornered a raccoon he'd been chasing. We were no longer the hunters.

"Maybe we better go sit on the deck," I answered. "It's a long story."

He glanced at his Rolex then looked over at Fred the same moment Bonnie let go of his collar. I thought Wilson was either going to spoil his pants or make a run for his car when Fred went over to sniff his boots.

"Maybe it's your boots he doesn't like," Bonnie said. "That's snake skin isn't it?"

"Crocodile. They're Ferrinis," he answered, sounding relieved when Fred lost interest and went to check out his SUV instead of attacking. "I'm supposed to meet the bookstore owner at eleven, so if it doesn't take too long, I'd love to hear what you were doing at Appleton's."

"This is a fantastic view you have. Is that Mount Evans?" Wilson asked, pointing toward the west once we were on my back deck. For a guy who was in a hurry a minute ago, he surprised me with his small talk. I had expected him to come straight to the point and ask why we were at Appleton's again.

I didn't have a chance to answer. Bonnie was in the kitchen with Fred and yelled through the open door, "Would you like coffee, Paul? Jake doesn't have anything cold to drink."

Old habits are hard to break. She was going through my refrigerator looking for the beer I used to stock by the case. I could have told her it was empty, but didn't think Wilson needed to know.

"No thanks. I've had my two cups for the day," he answered, unconsciously tapping his index finger on the deck table.

"So what brings you up here, Paul?" The annoying rat-a-tat-tat stopped.

Wilson stroked his goatee the way one would pet a cat, exposing a yellow nicotine stain between his index and middle finger. "Well, I remember at the signing, Ms. Jones mentioned you had a copy of *Tom Sawyer*, and I was wondering if I could look at it. You see, I'm a collector of rare books. Well actually, a dealer; I buy low and sell high. I would starve to death as an author if that was my only income."

"Isn't your book a best seller? I would think you made enough to retire."

"You wouldn't believe how many people think that. My publisher only pays twice a year, and the first payment won't be enough for a single car payment after they deduct their expenses and my advance."

"Wow, that's terrible."

"Live and learn. Next time I'll skip the whole agent publisher route and do it myself. A lot of traditional authors are doing that now and making a fortune."

He was no longer looking at me. His eyes had drifted upward as though he were seeking confirmation from someone in heaven "Oh, well. I still have my day job. Speaking of which, could I take a peek at your copy of *Tom Sawyer*?"

"I *had* a copy. Appleton stole it from me nearly two weeks ago."

Wilson reached inside his sport coat and pulled out a pack of cigarettes, then looked up at me. "I'm sorry to hear that. I would have paid dearly for a first edition. Do you mind?"

"Yes, he does." Bonnie had joined us on the deck, holding a makeshift tray with three cups of coffee. "Jake doesn't smoke and doesn't like it when I do, so why don't you have a cup of coffee instead."

I don't have a serving tray and was surprised to see she had improvised with an old cookie sheet I didn't know I owned.

"Thank you," he said, putting the cigarettes back into his jacket while keeping one eye on Fred. "I suppose another cup won't hurt." His fingers went back to beating my table when he must have realized

Fred was more interested in the cookie sheet than taking a bite of him. Wilson's tapping started with his little finger then quickly tapped each one in succession until he got to his index finger. It was really getting to me.

The tapping stopped abruptly. "How did you know it was Appleton who broke into your house and stole your book?"

"I didn't at first. It wasn't until I saw his face on TV after he'd been found dead in his truck." It was a complete lie, of course. I wasn't about to confess to breaking into Appleton's *before* he was found dead.

"Is that why you were there, the day I drove by? To get your book back?"

"And some other stuff he took." He didn't need to know it was our second trip, and we were there to remove evidence of our first visit.

"What about you, Paul?" Bonnie asked. "What were you doing there?"

Wilson had begun to tap again, but stopped long enough to answer Bonnie. "I wanted to make another offer for his book. He turned me down the first time I called, so I was hoping he had a wife or girlfriend who might sell it to me."

Bonnie's eyes grew large, "You called him? How did you... Oh, the guest list."

Wilson smiled, and went back to stroking his goatee. "Yes, he put his number, but not his address on the list. I had a heck of a time putting a name to the face at the book signing."

I jumped in before she could ask another question. "Then why did you leave? I mean, if you drove all the way up there from Parker, why didn't you knock on his door instead of letting Fred chase you away?"

Fred raised his head at the mention of his name, but laid back down when Bonnie spoke. "How do you know that, Jake? How do you know he lives in Parker?"

Wilson looked like he was about to ask the same question, so I spoke first. "His bio on the book jacket. It said he lives in Parker, Colorado with his two cats. Maybe that's why Fred doesn't like him. He must smell the cats."

I took a sip of my coffee before getting back to my little interrogation. I felt like I must have been a cop in a past life. "So why did you drive off, Paul?"

"Your dog spooked me."

Everyone turned to look at Fred who had gone back to sleep at my feet. He looked as vicious as a wooly caterpillar. I tried my best to keep a straight face. What kind of sissy was this guy?

"Of course, I didn't know it was your dog at the time. Nor did I know he was a Golden. All I could think of was being attacked by a pit-bull. I didn't need another copy of *Tom Sawyer* that bad." He looked down at his coffee then added, "Would you happen to have any cream and sugar, Miss Jones?"

Bonnie smiled and got up to go back inside. "I saw some milk in there, but I know Jake doesn't use sugar. His wife made him give up anything that could aggravate his diabetes."

"I don't have diabetes, Bon."

"No, and she wanted to make sure you didn't catch it either. Isn't that why you quit drinking?" There was no sense telling her diabetes isn't a communicable disease. My interrogation was falling apart.

Wilson looked like he was enjoying our little discourse on my lack of sugar in the house. "I know what you mean; it runs in my family too. I think the milk will be just fine."

"She really looks out for you, doesn't she," he said after Bonnie went to fetch the milk.

"I guess so. Ever since my wife died, she's been watching out for me and Fred. Sometimes I don't know how I would have managed without her." I caught myself before getting too melancholy. Wilson was obviously making small-talk again for his tapping began again the moment Bonnie left us.

Once more, the tapping stopped abruptly. "Just between you and me, Jake, were you planning on stealing your book back?"

"Like I said, it's a long story. I had a run in with the creep after he stole my stuff. Fred and I spotted him at the hardware store when I was buying a door to replace the one he broke. That's how I knew for sure it was he who'd broke into my place. So, yes, I was prepared to do the same to him if it came to that, but we didn't have to. His door was wide open when we got there."

"Unless you want cottage cheese in your coffee, you're going to have to go without that milk," Bonnie said, returning empty handed.

Wilson had been about to say something before Bonnie interrupted. He looked up at her blankly with his mouth still open. Luckily for him we rarely had seagulls this far from open water.

"I think she's telling us my milk is sour. Sorry, Paul, the power was off for a few days after that last storm." Another lie, but again, he didn't need to know Excel had shut me down last month until I paid their ransom and had the power restored.

"Oh. Well, thank you, Miss Jones, but I do need to get going. I wasted too much of your time already," he said, rising from his chair. "There is one thing I do need to ask before I leave, the reason I came here in the first place."

This, I thought to myself, is where the salesman does the bait and switch. "Sure, Paul. Shoot."

He paused long enough to choose his next words carefully while stroking his goatee. "Evidently, those kids who fell to their death thought they'd solved the riddle."

"Then there is a *treasure*?" Bonnie cut in. She was pretty sharp for being sixty-nine. I hadn't caught the contradiction, but Wilson did.

"In the original news article. All I did was copy it to make my book more interesting. I really didn't believe it."

He cleared his throat before continuing. "Have you heard if the Park County Sheriff found anything in their backpack that might indicate the kids were searching for the treasure? I heard from a friend of mine who works for the county that you guys are some kind of key witnesses."

Wilson caught me off guard. I wondered if he suspected we were up there because of the code we found in Appleton's cabin. "No, they haven't told us anything," I said, hoping he didn't perceive my fear.

If he did, he didn't let on while looking at his watch. "Well, Jake, I guess I'm wasting your time and mine. I'm sorry about your copy of *Tom Sawyer*. I didn't know about your burglary."

He turned to Bonnie, and offered his hand. "Thank you for your hospitality, Miss Jones. I do need to get to my appointment at the bookstore, then back to Parker before the traffic on C470 gets too bad."

"You better let me walk you out," I said, looking at his boots. "My guard dog might think those crocodiles are out to get him."

Fred was waiting by the door. He started to growl until I told him to hush. He let Wilson pass then followed us to the car.

Wilson handed me a business card before getting into his SUV. "I'd appreciate any information you get on those kids. It might help if the parents do decide to sue me." He quickly powered up his window when Fred gave one last bark.

"You don't like him much, do you, fella?" I asked, still holding his collar as Wilson drove away.

CHAPTER TEN

I wanted time to think after Wilson left, so I took Fred for a late walk around the lake. To be polite, I asked Bonnie to join us, hoping she would refuse. Hope is for the hopeless.

We were halfway through our walk when I made the impetuous decision to hike the Dedissee Trail to Three Sisters Park. The hike was over a mile long, and I began having second thoughts when Bonnie needed to catch her breath by taking a cigarette break.

"We can turn back, Bon, but we passed the halfway point, so you might be better off if I go back for my Jeep by myself after we get to the park."

"You can't drive a Jeep on this trail, silly. You'll get arrested."

"Now who's being silly? I'll take the highway to Buffalo Park Road. It's a paved highway all the way."

She seemed to consider it for a minute before crushing her cigarette in the dirt. "No, I'll be fine. But I fail to see why you want to go there in the first place. Appleton's truck and body are long gone by now."

A mountain bike came whizzing by before I could answer. "Hey, watch it you creep!" Bonnie yelled after the reckless rider.

I'd forgotten how dangerous our hiking trails could be with all the spandex clad mountain bikers from Denver. Luckily, Fred had left the trail when we'd stopped to rest, or he might take off after the idiot.

Two cigarette breaks later, and a half dozen near collisions with jerks who had no regard for hikers, we made it to the parking lot where I found the oil leak I had hoped for. The problem was, I found several oil spots. Any one of them could have been left by the Datsun, but more likely, they were from any of a thousand vehicles that visited the park on a daily basis. Unless I knew exactly where Appleton's truck had been parked, I might as well be looking for the shortest straw in a haystack. I was explaining this to Bonnie as we sat on a bench watching all the people go by.

Several of them gave her a nasty look when they walked past us. There must have been a no smoking sign at the entrance that we never saw. I think I had read something about the ban because of a high fire danger. Not that it would have made a difference with her, anyway.

"I don't know what I thought, Bon. I had one of my epiphanies that made me sure the kids were somehow involved. Not in Appleton's murder, but working with him to find the treasure."

She stomped on her cigarette butt after another hiker gave her a dirty look. "We don't know he was murdered, Jake. The news said it was a suicide. I wish you could accept that."

Then I realized the hiker's dirty look wasn't intended for Bonnie. "Oh, he was murdered all right," I said, walking over to a doggie poop-bag dispenser on the post next to our bench. "And once the medical examiner says so, the cops will be all over his cabin looking for prints."

I decided to attach Fred's leash after cleaning up his mess. I didn't need any more trouble with the law at the moment, but I may have been too late. No sooner had I put the poop-bag in the trash next to the post, than a park ranger pulled up in her truck. I couldn't help but stare. She had the same red pony-tail sticking out the back of her ranger cap that Julie had the first time I saw her. But that's where the similarity ended. This gal was a good six inches shorter, and twenty pounds heavier.

She looked at me and Fred then went over to Bonnie. "I'm sorry, ma'am, but there is a no smoking ban in effect for all the county and state parks. I'll have to ask you not to light up again."

Bonnie slowly moved her foot to hide her last cigarette butt. "Where did you ever get that idea, Honey? I gave up smoking years ago."

The cute ranger smiled showing perfect, pearl-white teeth that only came from years at the orthodontist. "Then that's not your cigarette you're hiding under your foot?"

Bonnie turned red from being caught in a lie, but continued with the charade anyway and moved her foot. "My goodness! Where did that come from?"

The ranger turned to me, no longer smiling. "Please have your mother go to your car if she wants to smoke, sir. I'd hate to have to arrest a grandmother for starting a forest fire."

I didn't bother to correct her on my lineage. "Yes, ma'am. I wonder if I could ask you a question before you leave."

"Sure. That's what I do best. I really hate playing cop." Her attitude seemed to change immediately.

"There was a suicide here a couple days ago. Do you know where the guy's truck was parked?"

She studied me with the prettiest light-blue eyes I'd seen in a long time. I began to feel embarrassed. I could feel myself being attracted to this ranger who reminded me so much of my dead wife. "Did you know the deceased?"

"It was his cousin." Bonnie had read my hesitation and jumped in. I was relieved, for I could never think of white lies so quickly.

The ranger's face softened. "I'm sorry, sir. I'd be happy to show you."

The three of us followed her to a parking place at the end of the lot. It was the perfect place to commit a murder. The spot was nowhere near a hiking trail, nor was it close to any of the picnic areas. No one else was parked anywhere near it, much like it must have been when Appleton supposedly killed himself.

"This is where I found your cousin last week. I really am sorry, mister...?" she let the mister hang as a question, like she expected an answer.

"Martin. Jake Martin. And this is Bonnie, my good friend and neighbor."

The ranger looked horrified. "Oh, please excuse me, Bonnie. I just assumed..."

Bonnie chuckled and offered her hand. "We get that a lot. If I had a son, I'd want him to be just like Jake. You couldn't find a sweeter guy."

"My name's Christine, but everyone calls me Chris. And who is this handsome fella?" she asked, bending down to pet Fred.

"That's Fred," I answered. "Show her how you shake hands, Freddie."

Fred sat and extended his left paw while wagging his tail.

Chris squatted down to his level and returned the handshake, using her left hand to match Fred's. "Aren't you a smart doggie? I'll bet you've got your handsome owner well-trained, don't you?"

Was she flirting with me? I saw a ring on her wedding finger when she'd grasped Fred's paw, so I assumed she used that particular adjective to describe all men. Still, it made me uncomfortable, so I started to change the subject, but Bonnie cut me off. She must have picked up on it too.

"He sure does. Jake would make someone a good husband, he's even house trained."

Chris laughed. I couldn't help notice two small dimples holding the smile in place. "I better get back to my patrol, but if you need anything, you can call the Open Space number posted at the entrance and leave me a message."

Watching her walk back to her truck reminded me of Julie again. My melancholy quickly faded when Bonnie broke the spell. "Is this what we came for?" She was examining an oil slick in the space next to where Appleton's truck had been parked.

"Stay, Fred," I said, letting go of his leash and walking over to Bonnie.

She stuck her index finger in the oil then rubbed it between her finger and thumb. "It's not engine oil, that's for sure, and it is red. I wonder if there is any test they can do to match it to the Datsun?"

"How do you know that, Bon?"

"Greg never let anyone change his oil. I remember it was a lot thicker than this. I had a devil of a time getting his clothes clean."

I bent down and did the same test, only I had to grab Fred with my free hand before he did it too. I'd have to work on that 'stay' command later. "Yep, no doubt about it. Only I don't need a lab test to confirm it. I'm sure it was the Datsun."

She stood up slowly, making me realize she was in no shape to walk back to my Jeep. "And how did you come to that conclusion, Sherlock?"

"A couple clues, Miss Watson. First, the oil spot is close to the parking curb. That tells me the oil leak isn't from a transmission, which would be further back, it's coming from a power-steering pump. Second, it's fresh. Notice Fred's paw prints. He didn't leave any prints when he walked on the other spots. Those oil stains look like they've been cleaned by a street sweeper, so they must be much older."

Bonnie took Fred's head between her hands, giving him his favorite treat, an ear rub. "Good boy, Freddie. You just cracked another case."

Fred ate it up. I doubt he knew why he was getting the attention, but he loved it anyway. I didn't have the heart to tell him the case wasn't cracked. All he had done was confirm, at least to me, that the Datsun had been here.

Bonnie didn't argue when I insisted she wait on the bench while Fred and I went back to get the Jeep. I turned around to wave at the first bend in the trail before we would be out of sight. She was too busy lighting a cigarette to notice us.

"You going to call him and tell him about the Datsun, Jake?" Bonnie asked after I picked her up from the park.

"Not yet. Maybe when we give our statements, but then I doubt if Deputy White will be there."

She gave me her blank look then must have realized I misunderstood. "Not White, silly. Paul Wilson. You said he asked you to call him if you got any new information on the kids."

"I forgot all about him, Bon. No. I suppose I'll help him out if the parents sue him, but I don't see how keeping him in the loop is to anyone's benefit. We need to concentrate on finding more evidence to keep White off our backs."

"And Margot. Don't forget that lawyer of hers," she added.

"Who can forget Margot?" I said, in a sarcastic tone as I pulled into Bonnie's drive. "I've got to go into town on some personal business. Why don't you give that sister of yours a call in the meantime and tell her you don't need the lawyer? He's going to be nothing but trouble for us."

Bonnie looked over at Fred who had stuck his big head between us. "I think Fred would have a better chance of telling Margot to back off. Wouldn't you, Freddie?" she said before giving his head one last rub before heading for her house.

I felt bad for bringing up Margot and the statement again. It obviously ruined Bonnie's mood, but at least she didn't ask why I had to go into town. An idea came to me on the way back from the park that I didn't want to share with her, for I knew she would want to tag along. It was bad enough Fred would be in danger; I didn't need to take a chance on getting Bonnie hurt too.

CHAPTER ELEVEN

Cory and Jennifer's house was less than a block from Colfax. The old saying about birds of a feather came to mind. I saw beggars, drunks and prostitutes on almost every corner, despite the newer stores trying to reclaim the area.

I parked across the street from their house, and pretended to read a map. The yellow police tape and crime scene signs I expected to see didn't exist. Nor were there any police cars parked in the driveway. I even checked up and down the street thinking the house might be under surveillance by an undercover team. Nothing. There were no unmarked cars, no vans, nothing that television cops use during a stakeout. Maybe real cops used cameras or satellites instead.

What was I thinking? I could feel my heart racing and blood pressure rising. Who would take care of Fred if I got caught or had a heart attack? "Calm down, Jake," I said aloud.

Fred turned his head at an odd angle when I spoke. He had taken Bonnie's seat after we dropped her off, and had been sleeping up until I had turned off on Colfax. I'm sure he would tell me I was a fool if he knew what I had in mind, for my plan to check the kids' driveway for power-steering fluid started to look really dumb. Was it even necessary?

I had reasoned that since the Datsun was sitting in an impound lot and I couldn't check it for a power-steering leak, the next best thing was to look for indirect evidence. My chances of getting away with snooping were much better here than in some impound lot, but I couldn't simply walk over there and look for oil spots. Someone would surely see me, and my Jeep wouldn't be hard to trace. I doubt if there were fifty of the old Wagoneers still registered in Colorado. And what if the police did have the house under surveillance?

When Fred started whining to be let out, I had my answer. I drove back to Colfax and parked in Casa Bonita's lot. Fred and I could walk the three blocks back to the kids' house, pretending to be locals out for a walk.

We hadn't gone a block when an older couple stopped us. "What a good looking doggie. What's your name, big fella?" The old man was bent over like a cartoon caricature and wasn't much taller than Fred. He surprised me when he stuck his hand out to pet him, but then, Goldens seem to have that affect on people.

"Say hello to the nice man, Freddie."

"That's an odd name for a dog." It was the old guy's partner, who I assumed was his wife. The grip on her purse told me she still didn't trust me.

"My ex named him. My daughter had her heart set on a Ginger, so when I brought home a male instead of a female puppy, my ex called him Fred, after Fred Astaire."

She relaxed the grip on her purse and a smile began to form on her lips. "Now *that* was when they knew how to make movies, wasn't it, Bill?"

Her husband looked up from shaking Fred's paw. "Huh? Who's moving?"

She ignored him and directed her answer to me. "Are you new to the neighborhood? I don't think I've seen you before?" So much for being inconspicuous. Unless these two had a severe case of senility, they wouldn't have any problem whatsoever picking us out of a police lineup.

"No. The wife wanted to browse one of those second-hand stores on Colfax, and Fred needed some exercise."

"Well, be careful, young man. I'd hate to see that beautiful dog get hurt. The neighborhood isn't what it used to be. There was a time we didn't even lock our doors and knew all our neighbors. Now they come and go so quickly, we don't even know half their names."

"Like those kids who got killed down the street," Bill cut in. Obviously, his hearing was selective, like my father's used to be when he would tune out my mother's nagging.

I tried to act shocked. "Two kids on this block were killed?"

"On the next block, but it wasn't here they were murdered. Up in the mountains somewhere," said his wife, who evidently realized I wasn't a purse snatcher by now, as she no longer held onto hers with both hands.

"Cops all over the place," Bill said before his wife could finish. "They went door to door asking all kinds of strange questions."

Oh, how I wanted to ask what kind of questions. Luckily, I didn't have to. "Yeah, like had we noticed any suspicious activity," Bill's wife said.

"Any activity on this block is suspicious," Bill added before his wife had time to speak again. Like my own parents, these two must have been married forever. Either that or they were Siamese twins at one time, because they answered each other's questions like they were joined at the hip.

"Well, they were wasting their time, and that's exactly what I told the detective," the wife continued. "I told him it had to be somebody like that lady Mr. Renfield says did it because Shelia killed her daughter."

"Now, June, we don't know that. How could someone our age dump those kids in a mine?"

The wife, I now knew as June, gave her husband a look before continuing, the kind of look my sister used to give when she knew something I didn't. "She had an accomplice, that's how. Mary at the beauty parlor says she's been hanging out with a younger man who must have helped her. And Mary should know. Her son is a Jeffco deputy."

My eyes must have come close to popping out of their sockets. I prayed my blood pressure didn't complete my exposé by making my face red, too.

"This young man doesn't want to hear your beauty shop gossip."

Oh, but I did. I almost said so when her cell phone went off. She pulled out an ancient phone from her purse and flipped it open. I bit my tongue, waved goodbye, and left before I said something to incriminate myself.

My blood pressure was back to normal once Fred and I were within sight of the kids' house. I stopped to let Fred sniff a telephone pole between the street and sidewalk. I casually looked back up the street in time to see the couple turn the corner onto Colfax.

Fred spotted a stick on the grass and nearly pulled me off my feet when he jerked the leash to get the stick. That's when my plan came together. All I had to do was let Fred off his leash and pretend to play fetch. I'd throw the stick up the kids' driveway and follow Fred so I could check for oil leaks. It should look innocent enough to any nosy neighbors who might be watching as they'd think it was a badly aimed throw.

Unfortunately, my toss was way off. Instead of the stick landing in the driveway, it sailed over a short, chain-link fence, separating the drive from the backyard. Like the rest of the house, repairs were long overdue. The gate to the yard had been torn off and lying on the ground, so Fred ran past the spot I wanted to examine and into the yard when he went after the stick. He didn't seem to care that he was trespassing.

Pretending to tie my shoe, I stopped short of the fence, and kneeled down. Sure enough, there was a puddle of fresh, red oil less than a foot ahead of the darker spots left by the engine.

"Come on Fred. Get out of there," I called out, now that I found what we had come for. He ignored me and began rolling around on the ground.

"Get your butt over here right now!" This time I said it loud enough that the next door neighbor peeked out between her broken Venetian blinds.

Fred picked a great time to let his instincts take control. I knew there was either a dead animal or something that came out the rear of one. He could be totally disgusting when he wanted. I made a display of showing his leash, for the benefit of the neighbor, and went in the backyard to get him. That's when I saw he wasn't the creature I'd accused him of being. It wasn't a dead animal or some by-product of one.

Fred had the evidence Bonnie and I needed to avoid lethal injection.

He found a plastic garbage bag that had been torn open by a scavenger. The rotting garbage must have been irresistible to Fred. Rolling in foul-smelling feces might have been great to cover his ancestor's scent when hunting, but the only animal Fred hunted was a squirrel he couldn't catch, no matter how bad he smelled.

Instead of scolding him, I ended up giving him praise when I saw the green tee-shirt with a Marine Corp label and the name, Appleton, printed on it. It looked like it had been used to wipe up blood. I no sooner picked it up when Bonnie's manicure kit fell out. It had been wrapped up in the bloody shirt. At least I assumed it was hers. I noticed the initials, BMJ, printed in gold cursive on the case when I opened it. Inside the case were a small pair of scissors, a couple nail clippers, a tweezer, and some other tools I didn't recognize. It looked like everything a woman would need to trim her fingernails, except for a file.

Fred and I hadn't gone a block on our way back to my Jeep when I saw the neighbor who had been watching us, leave her house and knock on Renfield's door. It was time to start jogging. My mind screamed, run, but that would really make me look guilty, so I pretended I was giving my dog some exercise with a leisurely jog.

No one seemed to be following us, so when we got to Colfax I stopped jogging to catch my breath. Only then did I realize my charade had backfired when I saw several people waiting at a bus stop watching us. I realized no serious jogger in his right mind would be caught running in long Levis and hiking boots. The onlookers were probably wondering what I was running from. I prayed their bus would show up before the police did.

Fortunately, we only had another two blocks to go before we could get in our Jeep, and be out of there before Renfield or the police came looking for us. Unfortunately, that wasn't going to happen. I spotted a Lakewood police car blocking my Jeep once we passed the bus stop. The officer was standing by my car saying something into his portable radio.

I turned up Pierce Street and kept walking past the parking lot. I couldn't believe Renfield had called the cops already. How had he known what I was driving?

We stopped once we were out of sight behind the Dollar Store, hoping no one at the bus stop had seen me park the car half an hour ago. I wasn't too worried about the street people. Most of them probably had warrants of their own and wouldn't want anything to do with the police. Other than the bus people, my fear was that a customer, or staff member in one of the stores, would recognize me or Fred. They might deem it their civic duty to tell the cop they had just seen me walk by.

I waited a few minutes then peeked around the building. The cop was placing a ticket on the car next to my Jeep.

CHAPTER TWELVE

"I'll bet you were ready to wet your pants, Jake." Bonnie said when I told her about the Lakewood police officer the next morning. We were sitting on her deck drinking coffee, or I should say, I was drinking coffee. I had slept in and Bonnie already had her quota for the day, but insisted on making coffee, even though she didn't want any more, and Fred preferred water.

"I wouldn't go that far, but I did say a prayer."

"A prayer?"

"Yes, I promised God if he got me out of this one that I'd go to church every Sunday."

"And you've already broken your promise. Do you want to go to hell? You can't do that, Jake. You don't want to fool with the Lord."

"I'll start next week, Bon, I promise. Just as soon as I find a church that allows pets."

"Jake!"

"Okay. How about I join the church of C and E?"

"I never heard of that. Is it Christian?"

"Christmas and Easter, of course it's Christian."

Bonnie laughed. "You're incorrigible, Jake."

"You win, Bon. Wake me next Sunday and I'll go with you. I wouldn't want to spend eternity in hell when Julie's in heaven. I just hope Saint Peter lets Fred in, too."

Bonnie poured me more coffee from the carafe on the table then lit a cigarette. "Well, I'm glad Fred got my manicure kit back before the police found it."

I had told her how Fred found her kit, and about my paranoia about seeing the cop by my Jeep, but I never mentioned the conversation with Bill and June. I didn't want to upset her with beauty parlor gossip. It could have been from before Appleton confessed, for all I knew, and telling Bonnie that we were both suspects could wait until I checked it out.

"We need to tell them, Bon, or we will be guilty of withholding evidence. The fact that it was wrapped in Appleton's shirt should prove you had nothing to do with the murder."

Bonnie looked like she'd just felt a spider crawl up her leg. "Have you forgotten it was missing a file? What if it's my file that was used to kill Shelia? Please don't tell them about it, Jake. Please?"

"What if there are prints they can trace to the killer?"

"Oh my God! I never thought of that. Can they get prints off of glass?"

"Glass?" I asked, wondering what she was talking about.

"The file, Jake. It's glass." She stopped long enough to roll her eyes. "And my name, now that I think of it."

Suddenly her eyes lit up like one of those new LED light bulbs. "That means it wasn't my nail file that killed Shelia. My name is on the plastic handle. Margot had it ordered special for my sixty-ninth birthday. If it were my file, they would have arrested me by now."

Talk about being stuck between a rock and a hard place. I needed to tell the cops about the shirt before someone cleaned the garbage from the kids' yard and destroyed crucial evidence. It was against my better judgment, but I didn't have the heart to say no.

"Okay, I'll call in an anonymous tip telling them where to find the shirt, but I think we're making a big mistake by not telling them about the manicure kit."

"You left the shirt?"

"Of course I left the shirt. They would never believe I found it there otherwise."

She seemed to consider my statement before she spoke again. "I would have never thought of that. Are you sure you weren't a crook in a different life?"

When I only smiled and didn't say anything, she continued. "But why tell them anything? I don't see how that shirt proves anything."

"Remember when I thought Craig had an accomplice who must have picked him up from Three Sisters after he left Appleton there?"

"So?"

"There's a very good chance Cory was that accomplice. He practically lives next door to Craig, so they must have known each other. I'm sure forensics will match the blood on the tee-shirt to that on Appleton's deck."

I took a breath and drank my coffee before continuing. "That is, if Fred didn't contaminate the evidence when he rolled in all the garbage. There was some really stinky stuff in there."

Fred looked up, then laid his head back between his outstretched paws when I didn't acknowledge him.

Bonnie raised her cigarette to her lips, but paused before taking another drag. "I know you would like to see Renfield hang, but did you ever consider it was Cory and Jennifer who killed Shelia and Appleton? Why else would they have the bloody shirt and my manicure kit?"

I wanted to tell her about Jennifer's poetry, but then I'd have to mention the unborn child and Bonnie was already too upset. "Maybe Cory was keeping those for insurance, or blackmail. I don't know why, Bon. All I know is Jennifer had nothing to do with any of it."

Bonnie blew a perfect smoke circle and watched it float away. "Then how do you explain my manicure kit? I'll bet that little thief lifted it out of my purse at the signing. No, Jake, she's in it with that boyfriend of hers, or was. I keep forgetting they're both dead now."

I couldn't argue with her logic, and realized Jennifer's poetry may have affected my judgment. "Assuming you're right, and I'm not agreeing with you, I'm simply thinking out loud, let's say she *did* steal the kit from your purse. That would explain how it ended up in her trash. And if it was her and Cory who killed Appleton then there should be the telltale oil spot from the Datsun at his cabin."

Bonnie beamed like a child with a new toy. "We should check the cabin to see if the Datsun's been there."

"I suppose it won't hurt to drive by. We could stop on the way back from giving our statements."

"Do we have to, Jake?"

"It's already Tuesday; White isn't going to wait much longer."

"Let's go after we check out the oil spot. If we find one then maybe you can tell him about the shirt."

She had a point. There's no such thing as an anonymous tip since public phone booths went the way of Superman. All other phones can be traced. "No, not the shirt. I'll have to think of some other way they can discover it. Like I said they will think I planted it to cover our tracks at the cabin. I might as well walk in and sign a confession in triplicate."

We were almost to Conifer when I began to have my doubts; sooner or later the cops would be searching Appleton's cabin and asking his neighbors questions. We got lucky the first time we went there. The only person other than Margot who knew we were at the cabin was the author Paul Wilson, and he seemed to have bought my story.

I was driving Bonnie's Cherokee with her in the passenger seat and Fred's big head resting on the center divider. The rest of his body was in the back seat. "This is stupid, Bon," I said without taking my eyes off the road. "Someone might see us."

"I already took care of that, Jake. Why do you think my Cherokee is so dirty?"

"Because you went four wheeling yesterday?"

"No, silly. Because I made it look dirty. I'll finish the job just before we get there with a bucket of mud I brought along to complete the subterfuge. It's a trick Greg used to do, back when we were young and poor. He covered his plates with mud so the cops wouldn't see they were expired."

I had to smile. "My dad told me stories about doing the same thing, only it backfired on him. The cop who pulled him over said the mud was a red flag, and he would have never noticed the expired plate otherwise. It's the oldest trick in the book."

Bonnie thought about it for a while before answering. "Then I'll only cover a few numbers and leave the sticker visible."

"What do you think, Fred? Think the mud on the plate ploy will work?" Fred's head had been turning like a spectator at a tennis match. He followed whoever was speaking at the moment. When he answered by barking once, I took it as a yes. Sometimes I think he actually understands what we are talking about.

We pulled over at the Pine Junction Country Store so Bonnie could run in for cigarettes while I smeared mud on the plates. She stopped before getting out and turned to me. "Are you going to tell White if we find the Datsun was there? I mean, it would prove the kids knew Appleton, and if the blood on the shirt is his, well then..."

"The kids probably killed him," I finished her thought after she paused too long. "I should, but then I'd have to tell him about our little break-in. No, we'll just have to hope their forensics can put the pieces together after they find the shirt."

"Thanks, Jake. Margot would kill me if you told White without her lawyer present," she said before going into the store.

The only other person in the parking lot held the door for her then followed her inside. It was my chance to cover the plates. I didn't leave any numbers visible because it wasn't going to fool the police, and I didn't want any nosy neighbors getting a partial.

Bonnie laughed at me when I turned onto Appleton's road and told her I had heard of cases where they traced a car with only one letter or number by matching it with the make and model. She started to say something about my imagination when we saw several sheriffs' vehicles and a CBI truck in Appleton's drive. I kept on going, hoping they didn't notice the mud on our plates.

"Wow, that was close," I said after parking around the bend where we couldn't be seen. I left the engine running in case we had to make a quick getaway.

She had her pack of cigarettes out and was playing with the seal. "Did you see that huge truck? What on earth do you suppose that is?"

"CBI, according to the sign on the door."

"It took them long enough," she said.

I put the Jeep back in gear and slowly pulled back onto the road. "Lucky for us. If they hadn't been sidetracked by the fake suicide, they might have sent the forensics' team out before we had a chance to wipe our prints."

Neither of us spoke again until I was back at the intersection of 285 and waiting for the light to turn. It had taken a little time to find a road that didn't go past Appleton's cabin. I tried using Lucy, my GPS, but would have had better luck asking Fred. I gave up after Lucy couldn't get a signal, and stumbled on to Highway 74, which I knew would take us to 285.

"Let's forget about giving any statement today, Bon. Maybe you need Margot's lawyer after all," I said, pulling out into traffic when the light finally changed.

She put the pack of cigarettes she had been holding back in her purse. "You won't get any argument from me."

I was about to answer but was side-tracked when I noticed a semi-truck in my rear-view mirror barreling down on us. The driver had run a red light, and was about to turn us into road kill. I couldn't switch lanes because another car was already in the fast lane, so I quickly swerved toward the shoulder and came to a stop.

Bonnie waved a single finger and yelled out a few choice words to the reckless driver when he went speeding by.

I crossed myself before turning to her. "This is one time I don't care if you smoke the whole pack, Bon. What was that guy thinking?" I asked before turning around to check on Fred.

"Oh, crap. That's all we need now." Fred was fine, but pulling in behind me was a State Patrol car with its lights flashing.

CHAPTER THIRTEEN

By Wednesday, the three of us were on our way to Bailey to give our statements of what we had seen on Mosquito Pass. I had nearly forgotten about the ticket the cop gave me for driving with expired plates. He said he wouldn't have noticed if they hadn't been covered in mud. It seems Bonnie was eighteen days past the grace period of getting her plates renewed.

This time we took my Jeep to avoid another ticket. I waited until we were on the road before telling Bonnie I was going to tell Deputy White about the bloody shirt and our visit to the cabin.

"You should have said something sooner, Jake. Margot will have a cow. You know I can't do that without her lawyer." Bonnie fumbled through her purse, looking for her phone. "I better call her and see if Harvey can meet us there."

It would be useless to try to stop her, assuming she found her cell phone. I had seen her miss more than one call when she couldn't get to it in time. "Harvey must be far too busy to just drop everything and drive to Bailey, but I suppose it's worth a try."

She held a finger to her lips in the universal sign for me to shut my mouth. "Damn it, Margot, answer your phone."

Her sister's phone did as it was told and came back with a recorded message.

Bonnie yelled into her phone, "Margot, call me back when you get this. It's important!" Then she slammed the flip-phone shut and looked at me with real fear in her eyes.

"Can't we do this later, Jake? Please?"

"Are you forgetting the cops at Appleton's yesterday? It can only mean one thing."

She cut me off before I could finish. "They no longer think he killed himself."

"Exactly, and no matter how clever we thought we were, they are bound to find something to connect us to the crime scene."

Bonnie looked at her phone again before putting it back in her purse. "Like Fred's paw prints," she said. "Okay, Jake, you win. I suppose Margot can always bail me out if she has to."

We rehearsed our story during the forty-five minute ride, so if we wouldn't be caught in a lie if we got interrogated separately. It was a simple story. It was basically the one we told Wilson, without the part of us breaking and entering Appleton's cabin.

"Be a good boy, Freddie. We shouldn't be long," I said after parking the Jeep and rolling down all the windows.

Bonnie didn't make a move to get out. "Maybe I should stay here with him, Jake."

"It's not even seventy, Bon. He'll be fine."

"No. Not the heat. What if they arrest us? Who's going to take care of Fred?"

"Unless the deputies drive unmarked cars, the answer is no one. There are only two cars in the parking lot, and not one of them is a police vehicle or has county plates."

Once we left the building, I realized my observation had been correct. The only officer at the substation was a clerk, and she was busy with someone paying a ticket. I grabbed Bonnie's elbow and led her back outside.

"Change of plans, Bon," I said after we were back at my Jeep. "Let's just give them a statement on what we saw and did on Mosquito Pass."

Bonnie looked relieved. "Okay with me. I wasn't looking forward to spending the night in jail anyway. What made you change your mind?"

"What did you see in there?"

"Nothing. Just someone paying a ticket."

"Exactly. No deputies. I doubt if they have six in the entire county. They have to be way too busy to bother trying to catch us in a lie, so there's no need in asking for trouble."

The drive home was quiet, at least our conversation was. Margot called back before we got half a mile from the sheriff's substation. I became invisible while Bonnie reassured her sister everything was okay, and they went on to talk about nothing that interested me. I waited until she hung up before saying anything.

"How well do you know your Bible, Bon?"

She looked at me wide-eyed. "What?" Then she seemed to understand. "Oh, you mean for church next Sunday."

"Not exactly. I had something a little more devious in mind. I was thinking of knocking on a few doors in Appleton's neck of the woods. I could dress Fred as a seeing-eye dog and pretend to be a blind Jehovah's Witness. Of course, I'd need your help to pull it off."

"That's got to be the goofiest idea you've ever had," she said, once she'd finally stopped laughing.

"We need to know what the cops found at Appleton's. Maybe one of the neighbors would open up to a couple of bible-toting evangelists, especially if one of them was blind. So unless you have a better idea, I think I need to start looking for one of those harnesses guide dogs wear."

"How would they know what the sheriff found in the cabin? It seems to me that if the cops found anything they'd keep it to themselves." She looked at me like I'd lost it.

"True, but bear with me for a minute. What if the cops went around interviewing the neighbors after searching the cabin? It's possible they might have said something about what they found."

Bonnie's vacant stare answered my question without her having to say a word.

"Yeah, you're right, Bon. Dumb idea. Besides, I doubt if Fred could pull it off anyway. They'd know he wasn't a service dog the first time he saw a cat or squirrel."

"Well, you did have one good idea today. I'm glad you changed your mind about confessing. Margot would have been madder than a horny hornet if I confessed without her lawyer present." She absentmindedly turned her phone over and over again. "What really made you change your mind anyway? I'm not buying that it was because they don't have the manpower to waste on us."

"Who were we going to tell? The only one in the office was the clerk. I really need to talk to Deputy White before I go confessing to breaking and entering."

She looked at her phone like she'd just realized what it was. "What about Margot? Should I call her back and ask her to send Harvey with us when we talk to White?"

"You can call her if you want, but tell her you won't need her lawyer because there's no need to involve you in this. I'll tell White it was just me and Fred at the cabin. I'm pretty sure his paw prints are the only prints the CBI will find. I'm positive they will never know you were there."

Bonnie had put the phone away and replaced it with a pack of cigarettes as I pulled into her driveway. "I can't let you take all the blame. No jury in the world is going to convict an old widow pushing seventy. Please let me go with you when you talk to White. I promise not to tell Margot until afterwards."

She got out of the Jeep, lit a cigarette and took a deep drag. "I'd like to meet your mama someday, Jake, and tell her what a great job she did raising you." The smoke must have gotten in her eyes, for I thought I saw her wipe a tear from her face.

CHAPTER FOURTEEN

Deputy White was waiting at the substation for us Thursday morning. He had returned my call the previous night and agreed to meet us. This time I left Fred home so if we did get arrested, he wouldn't get lost in some animal shelter.

His truck was parked next to the car we had seen when we gave our statements earlier. "I wonder if they have a jail cell here?" I asked Bonnie after shutting off my engine.

She was playing with her cigarette pack again, a sure sign she was nervous. "Do you think they'll arrest us?"

"Sorry, I was just thinking out loud. I noticed his truck isn't set up to transport prisoners, so I was wondering where they kept them until they could send them to Fairplay."

Bonnie lit a cigarette once she was out of my Jeep. "I need a minute before we go in there, Jake. You should have let Harvey come with us."

"All the more reason you need to stay here and let me go in alone."

She dropped her cigarette and stomped on it. "No, I'm just as guilty as you. The Lord would never forgive me if I didn't own up to my sins." She didn't wait for a response and headed toward the building.

It was all I could do to catch up with her at the door. "Okay, Bon, but let me do the talking," I said, opening the door for her.

We were led to a back office by the clerk where Deputy White was waiting for us.

"So what is so important that I had to drive all the way in from Fairplay?" he asked after the preliminary greetings were over and we'd taken two chairs in front of his desk.

"We saw your CSI team yesterday, or whatever you call it."

White had a smile that would put Bozo the Clown to shame. "Tell me something I don't already know."

"You knew we were there?" Bonnie asked.

"I thought I recognized that Cherokee from the time I was at your place, so I ran a check on it and guess who got a ticket not a mile away?"

Evidently it was a rhetorical question, as he didn't wait for an answer. "So what were you doing there?"

Bonnie answered for me. "Jake wanted to check for power-steering fluid in the driveway."

He looked briefly at her before turning to me. "Is that why I had to drive all the way from Fairplay, Jake?" I knew the tone in his voice from when I was a kid. My father had used that tone after I'd been caught smoking in the boy's restroom at school. When I got home, he asked me how was school. He never asked before, so I confessed thinking he already knew.

"It's true. I wanted to see if Cory's Datsun had been there, but it's not the first time. We were at Appleton's cabin before he was found dead, and I took a shotgun he had stolen from me." I wanted to add that Bonnie had not gone inside, but didn't want to be caught in a lie if they had found her prints.

"So you're telling me you two committed a felony breaking and entering, and decided to come clean after driving by Appleton's cabin yesterday when you saw the forensics truck?"

"No, sir, Bonnie was just an innocent bystander, and I didn't break in. The door was wide open and when I saw my gun on his kitchen table...well it did belong to me, so I wasn't really stealing."

I expected the deputy to act surprised, but he only smiled. "You should have called me before taking anything. But I suppose I would have done the same under the circumstances."

"Then you're not upset that we entered a crime scene?"

"I would be if it was a crime scene," White answered.

"Tell him about the blood on the deck, and the shirt Fred found, Jake."

I bumped her knee in a futile attempt to shut her up.

"Jake thinks you should run a DNA test on the blood samples to see if they match. He thinks those kids killed Appleton, don't you, Jake?"

White was no longer smiling. "I know about the blood on the deck. What's this about a bloody shirt? Did you remove evidence we should have found?"

"Not at the cabin, silly. Fred found it at the kids' house," Bonnie said.

White's mood changed for the worse. "Who the hell is Fred?"

"He's Jake's dog," she answered, then followed it with an Ow when I bumped her knee a little too hard.

I ignored Bonnie's cry and tried my best to stay focused on White. "I'm sorry, Deputy, I think I better start from the beginning and tell you everything."

White was all smiles again after I explained my adventure at Cory and Jennifer's house, and how Fred had found Appleton's shirt after rolling in the trash. I didn't mention Bonnie's manicure kit, but I did tell him how scared I was when I saw the Lakewood cop giving the car next to my Jeep a ticket. I think that's what made him grin. Then I told him about our trip to Three Sisters Park.

"We saw the same oil spot next to where he supposedly shot himself. That's why we went back to his cabin. We wanted to see if the kids had left their calling card in his driveway, too."

"That they did. A rather large spot indicating they had been there for some time, but what makes you think Appleton was shot?" White asked rather smugly.

"He wasn't shot?" Bonnie asked, placing a hand on her knee and leaning forward before asking the question.

Now I was the one with big eyes. "But you said you found power-steering fluid in the driveway. That proves Cory was there and if the blood on the deck matches the shirt, he must have shot Appleton at the cabin and moved the body to Three Sisters to make it look like a suicide."

"This is why you two need to leave detective work to the pros. The blood on the deck that you think belongs to Appleton isn't human, and he killed himself with a bad injection of heroine, not a gunshot."

"You're telling us it was an accident? What about the note where he confessed to killing Shelia?" I asked.

"I didn't say it was an accident. You didn't hear it from me, not that it matters once the press finds out, but he overdosed on purpose."

White got up from his chair, indicating he was done. "The only crime I see is when you entered his cabin, but I'll let it go if you two promise to quit playing detective."

Except for small talk about Bonnie not having to get her sister involved, we hardly spoke on the trip home until she had me pull over at the liquor store in Evergreen. I waited in my Jeep while she went in for cigarettes. She surprised me when she came out with a shopping bag.

I got out and opened her door. Any other time she would object to anyone holding a door for her, but it was either that, or she would have to put the bag down and open it herself.

"I didn't want to drink alone, Jake, so I got you a six-pack of your favorite beer," she said.

I took the bag until she got in. "Thanks for thinking of me, Bon, but you know I gave it up for Julie."

She looked up at me, and I gave her the bag. "Trust me. After today, she won't mind if you have a couple."

I must admit it was tempting, but I simply smiled and shut her door.

She waited until we were back on the road before speaking again. "We just admitted to breaking and entering and got off with only a warning. I don't know how you can celebrate without a little drink."

"I'm afraid it's not quite over, Bon. Did you forget about your manicure kit?"

"I don't follow, Jake. You got it back from those kids so how could the police trace me now? You don't think they still suspect me, do you?"

"Deputy White doesn't because it's not his case. Shelia wasn't murdered in Park County, but you can bet your next Social Security check the Lakewood police haven't forgotten about that nail file."

"But they would have arrested me by now if it was my file. My name is on the handle."

"Okay, you got me there. I was sure it was Appleton who killed Shelia and hid the evidence in the kids' trash. But it couldn't be your file, not if your name is on it."

"How do you figure it was Appleton? I thought you said it was Craig?"

"That was before I found your manicure kit in the trash. Let's suppose Appleton broke into her place looking for her copy of *Tom Sawyer* when she was doing her nails. She screams when she sees him, then he grabs the file out of her hand and stabs her in the neck. He gets blood all over his shirt from the wound, so he takes off his shirt, grabs the manicure kit and throws everything in the nearest trash can when he leaves."

Bonnie rolled her eyes. "And what was Shelia doing with my manicure kit in the first place? And why would Appleton want to hide it anyway?"

"I don't know. Maybe White is right and we need to leave it to the pros. None of it makes any sense to me. When the cops find Appleton's prints on the file you'll no longer be a suspect and the case will be closed." I said as I pulled into her driveway.

Bonnie fiddled with her pack of cigarettes. It was obvious she couldn't wait to get out of my Jeep and light up. "Good idea, Jake. Now go get Freddie and come back down so we can celebrate."

Fred acted like I'd been gone a month. He was still trying to get me to play with him long after we'd left our cabin and walked down the path to Bonnie's. I quit throwing Fred's stick when we started up her deck stairs for fear he might jump off the deck to retrieve it, but it didn't stop him from trying to put it in my hand.

Bonnie was sitting on her porch rocker staring at her drink as if hypnotized and didn't look up when I spoke. "Are you okay, Bon?"

I had caught her rubbing her chest and her face looked like she was in pain, but she smiled when she saw Fred.

"It's that damn sister of mine. She's all ticked off because I went without her lawyer," she answered reaching out to pet Fred. "You must be starving, Freddie. Would you like Aunt Bonnie to get you something?"

"Please don't bother, Bon. I think you need to go inside and lie down. We can celebrate some other time."

She got up and started to go inside. "Nonsense, it's just a little heartburn. Now sit down while I get us something to eat." She went back inside before I could beg off. Fred understood the word 'eat', for he quit trying to put the stick in my hand, and started wagging his tail.

I opened a soda she had left for me on the table, and tried to think of a nice way to tell her we wouldn't be staying for dinner. She may no longer be a suspect in Shelia's murder, but it didn't get me any closer to finding Julie's ring and copy of *Tom Sawyer*. I needed to go while there was still enough daylight for me to sneak back to Appleton's cabin and retrieve my property.

Fred couldn't care less about my plans and went to Bonnie's screen door. At first I thought he must have smelled her cooking something good until he started barking at me. "What's wrong, Freddie?"

He ran over to me, barked again, and then ran back to the screen door.

I knew Fred better than any human. "Bonnie, are you okay in there?" I asked, getting up from my chair.

"Oh my God! Bonnie!" I yelled when I saw her lying on the floor.

CHAPTER FIFTEEN

Margot and her son, Jonathan, were already at the hospital waiting room when I arrived. I had called Margot right after the ambulance left, and then rushed down the mountain leaving Fred home alone. They couldn't have beat me there by more than a few minutes, for I saw a young Hispanic man get up and offer his chair to Margot when I walked in. All the others were taken.

"Hello, Margot," I said after walking over to her. Then I turned to Jonathan, but before I could do more than nod my head, Margot spoke.

"I suppose we should thank you for saving Bonnie's life." Her makeup was smeared from wiping her eyes with the handkerchief she had in her hand.

"Thank the 911 operator. She told me how to give Bonnie CPR until the ambulance arrived. It's what kept her alive until the paramedics took over."

Jonathan looked up from the cell phone he had been texting with, despite the signs asking visitors to turn off their electronic devices. "We wouldn't have to thank anyone if you hadn't gotten her so upset.

What kind of neighbor are you? Walking in here like everything is fine and dandy. You didn't even ask how she's doing."

My first instinct was to tell him where he could put his cell phone, but I didn't want to make any more of a scene than necessary. Evidently, we had become better entertainment than the magazines that people near us were reading. They didn't even bother to pretend they weren't listening.

"I asked at the desk. They said she's going to be okay."

"Why wouldn't you let me get my lawyer involved instead of making her face the police by herself?" Margot asked. "She's nearly seventy years old, my God. I'm surprised she didn't die during the interrogation."

I felt a rage building inside of me that counting to a hundred wouldn't quell. They had just accused me of giving Bonnie a heart attack. Now I knew why Cain had killed his brother. But when I looked down to tell Margot off, I couldn't. After she had wiped off her smudged make-up, she looked just like Bonnie. The only difference between the twins was their hair color.

"I'm sorry, Margot. I had no idea she had a heart condition."

Her eyes darted from me to someone at the receptionist's desk. She was so obvious that both Jonathan and I turned to look. A uniformed police officer had been talking to the receptionist and turned to look our way at the same time we had turned to look in his direction. Jonathan quickly looked away.

The officer left the desk and made his way over to us through the crowd. "Mrs. Scott?"

Margot looked horrified. "Yes?"

"Mrs. Scott, I need to ask you a couple questions about your sister. Would you mind following me to the hospital's security office? It's just down the hall." Now we had the attention of every person in the room, and no one pretended to read their magazines anymore.

Margot got up slowly and turned to her son. "Jon, you better go with me."

"I'm sorry, ma'am, I need to speak to you alone."

It was all he needed to say. Suddenly, the color was back in her face and the old Margot was back. "It's either my son or my lawyer. I'll let you choose."

"Uh, well I guess it will be okay."

She turned to me. "Come and get me if you hear anything before this keystone cop is finished, will you, Jake?" She said it so nicely that no one would have guessed she had just chewed me up and spit me out. "I'll leave word at the desk to get you if the doctors come out before I get back." Her face exposed her joy of being in charge again; she had that smug smile that set her apart from her sister.

Margot and Jon weren't gone five minutes before a nurse came looking for me. "Mr. Martin?" I could tell without asking that it was good news. I spent enough time in hospitals last year when Julie was dying to be able to read a nurse's face.

"Yes."

"Mrs. Jones would like to see you."

I had expected to see tubes sticking out of Bonnie's head like a mythological hydra. All she had were a few wires leading from something in her gown pocket to the inside of the gown. She wasn't even hooked up to an IV.

"How you doing, Bon Bon?" I asked with a forced smile. "Fred said to say hi, and wants to know when you'll be home to feed him your leftovers."

She wanted to answer, but her tears wouldn't let her. I cautiously reached out for her hand to hold it, and waited for the tears to stop.

"What the hell are you doing in here?" Margot had thrown open the curtain that separated Bonnie from the other ER patients, and she was furious.

"I told you to come and get me! Haven't you done enough damage for one day?"

The policeman from the waiting room was standing behind her, so I didn't bother to tell her off. Instead, I turned back to Bonnie without answering. "I better be going, kid. Freddie will be happy to hear you're doing so well."

I gave Bonnie's hand a little squeeze and stood up to face her sister. "Please call me with her room number when they move her, Margot. I'd like to send some flowers to cheer her up."

"Like hell I will! Get out of here before I have you arrested."

Jonathan didn't see me when I walked past the waiting room. His thumbs were working the virtual keyboard of his cell phone and it took all his attention. I wanted to ask him what the police had to say, but didn't need another confrontation so I kept on going.

I tried to call Bonnie the minute Fred woke me, but had to wait. Margot had left instructions at the switchboard not to put me through, or give me Bonnie's room number. If she didn't call me soon, I would call back pretending to be Jonathan.

Fred didn't seem to mind that my scrambled eggs were no match for Bonnie's. He scarfed them down, his and mine, even though they were burned beyond recognition, and wanted back out before I could finish my first cup of coffee.

I checked the time on my cell phone while watching Fred sniff ground he had smelled a thousand times. It was too soon to impersonate Jonathan, so I decided to sit out on my back deck with my notebook and do some work. No sooner had I sat down than I saw a car on the lower part of the road.

With only four other houses on Columbine Circle, I rarely see any traffic, so it's always a good excuse to stop writing whenever a car drives by. However, this time I didn't recognize the car that pulled into Bonnie's drive. Fred must have heard it too, and was now barking to be let back in. I ignored Fred and waited to see who got out of the car.

Bonnie's house was just too far away to make out the driver, other than it was a woman. The same was true for the car. I could see it was a dark blue, or black, late-model crossover, but that's all I recognized. Ever since someone got the great idea to mate an SUV with a mini-van, I haven't been able to tell one from another. I lost sight of it after she parked in the driveway, but saw her again when she started up Bonnie's front stairs. Unless it was a guy in drag, there was no doubt that the driver was a woman. She was short with gray hair and wasn't more than a couple feet taller than the stair railing.

She disappeared again when she reached the deck and headed for Bonnie's front door. Usually, it is possible to hear people talk on the lower road, so listening for Bonnie's bell, or a knock on the door wasn't out of the question. Fred ruined that for me with his insistent barking to come in.

I gave up trying to listen and went to let Fred in. He looked at me, barked, and ran down the stairs when I opened the door. "It's not Bonnie, Freddie, but let me put on some shoes and we'll go down there and see who it is." He seemed to understand, and sat without another bark.

We should have gone straight down the path between the two houses, as it was the shortest and quickest route, but I didn't want to be seen trespassing in case the woman had been sent there by Margot. I would have to stay on the road and take the long way down to her house. All I got for being so cautious was a glimpse of the woman's car in a cloud of dust when we finally made it to the lower road.

Fred and I continued on the road until we reached Bonnie's house. He ran up her stairs to the front door, so I followed. I checked the lock and peeked in the windows while he paced back and forth sniffing for odors undetectable to the human nose. The door and windows were secure and nothing I could see through the windows seemed to be out of place. We left taking the shortcut up the hill to call Bonnie. That's when I found out why the Lakewood cop had wanted to talk to Margot.

CHAPTER SIXTEEN

Beethoven was playing on my cell when Fred and I made it back to my cabin. Bonnie had left several messages for me to call her back. I punched in the hospital's number after listening to the first message and heard the urgency in her voice.

"Jake! Where have you been? I've been trying to get you all morning," she said when she heard my voice.

"I'm sorry, Bon. Fred and I went on a walk around the circle. You know what lousy reception we get up here. I didn't get your calls." I neglected to tell her why we went on the walk. "How are you doing? I wanted to check earlier but figured you needed your rest."

"Don't worry about this old broad. It'll take more than a little heart attack to keep me down."

"So it *was* a heart attack?"

"So they say. They also say you saved my life. I don't know how…"

Her voice broke up, and I thought I heard a muffled sob. "Bon, are you sure you're okay?"

I waited what seemed like minutes for her to come back on the line. In reality, it was only a few seconds, but if I were a nail biter, my fingers would have been bleeding.

"Oh, Jake, I hate to ask you this after you've done so much for me, but I think they're going to arrest me."

"Is that why the cop was there? To arrest you?"

"No. He wanted to know if I had a personalized manicure kit. I need you to get the kit from my bedroom and put it someplace where it can't be found."

"Did he mention your initials on the file?"

"No, but I'll tell you, Jake, I came this close to confessing."

I could imagine her holding her thumb and index finger to the phone. "Well, don't you worry, that kit is as good as gone once I get back inside. Do you still hide your key under the flowerpot on the porch where every burglar would look? I locked up after the paramedics left."

I thought I heard a stifled laugh. "Yes, silly. Can you…"

"That's not Jake, I hope." It was Margot's unmistakable voice.

"I've got to go now, Patty. Thanks for calling," Bonnie said before the line went dead.

Fred and I went back down to Bonnie's the minute she hung up. It was reasonable to assume the police might get a warrant to search her house for the manicure kit, so I needed to get it before they did. We were down the path and up her stairs in record time. Fred must have thought I wanted to play, for he hadn't seen me run so fast since he was a puppy. He nipped at my heels on the way down, nearly tripping me. He was the first one up the stairs, and I expected him to continue the game he liked to play of pretending he was a fierce guard dog and growl at me when I would come up our stairs, but this time he lost interest in the game and was sniffing the flower pot. I tensed up when I saw the circular stain where the pot had been. Someone had moved it.

I tried in vain to remember if I had seen the stain earlier. Was it the old lady who moved it? I peeked through the beveled glass window of the door in case she had brought someone with her I hadn't seen; someone she dropped off to do the dirty work, while she drove away to divert suspicion. My heart was beating so fast that I was sure whoever might be in there could hear it.

Then Fred, who had lost interest in the flower pot's new location, turned and barked. The bark was short and to the point, not his repetitive alarm bark, but his, "What's up?" bark.

I held a single finger to my lips, telling him to be quiet, and went back to checking for the intruder. The beveled glass made it too blurry to see inside, so I slowly crept over to the next window. I saw nothing unusual, and no movement inside, so I went over to the flower pot. I half expected the key to be missing, but it was there when I looked under the pot. Perhaps it was one of the paramedics who had moved it, and my paranoia had gotten the better of me.

"Stay out here, Freddie, and warn me if anyone shows up," I said, turning the key in the lower lock; the one I had set from inside before closing the door after they took Bonnie away. But the door still wouldn't open. Someone had used the key to lock the deadbolt. It could only mean that the old lady had moved the pot, used the key to gain entry, and locked everything after she left. Which also meant, she had to know the key was there in the first place.

Once inside, I went to Bonnie's bedroom where she said I would find the manicure kit in her top vanity drawer, wrapped in a plastic grocery bag. She had one of those old vanities you see on late-night television shows from the thirties. It was complete with a round mirror and little padded stool. I quickly looked in the mirror to see if I was being watched. That, too, was something I'd seen in one of those black and white movies.

Relieved, but disappointed the trick didn't work when the only apparition I saw was myself, I opened the top drawer. Bonnie's kit was there, exactly where she said it would be. I opened it half expecting to see her nail file, or what was left of it. In the back of my mind I imagined the old, gray haired lady had planted the broken handle where the police could find it.

I took the kit and checked the rest of the house looking for the file in case Gray Hair put it somewhere else. I looked in the dresser drawers, the bathroom, and even under the bed, but found nothing. If it was here, she did a great job of hiding it.

My next stop was the kitchen, where I knew Bonnie kept a box of doggie treats for Fred. I didn't think she would miss one or two. I was ready to leave with Fred's biscuits when I saw a copy of *Tom Sawyer* on the table. That was weird, for Bonnie never mentioned having a copy. It had to have been put there by the intruder, and the only reason I could think of was that I had been right about someone trying to frame Bonnie. I stuffed the book in the plastic bag with the manicure kit, and was about to leave when I noticed the sink cabinet was slightly ajar.

Bonnie always chided me about leaving cabinet doors open, so it struck me as odd that she would do it herself. I went over to close it, and discovered it was the trash can she kept there that was keeping the door open. I looked inside and saw a blood-soaked, paper towel. Inside the towel was the broken, glass handle from Bonnie's nail file. Even without the benefit of six years of college, I knew it was hers, because her name was printed on the protective sleeve.

Fred was waiting quietly when I came back out. To my surprise, it looked like he was obeying orders and sitting where he could see anyone coming up the road. "Good, boy," I told him, and gave him one of Bonnie's treats.

It was gone in a millisecond and he looked up at me begging for more. He ate the second one even faster, but instead of asking for another, he turned toward the road and cocked his head to the side. I couldn't hear anything, but I could see a big cloud of dust down toward Upper Bear Creek Road. Someone was headed our way. I didn't have to guess who. If the book had been left to frame Bonnie, it would be the cops with a search warrant.

We made it back to our cabin in time to see two sheriff's SUVs pull into Bonnie's drive.

My first instinct was to hide the evidence in my cabin, but the devil's advocate inside my head whispered that my place was probably next on the sheriff's search list. Fred and I could try to make our escape in my Jeep, but the voice in my head said I'd be caught before I got off our road. Fred solved my dilemma by running toward the trail leading up our little mountain. The hill behind my cabin was part of the Denver Parks system. Technically, it was out of the jurisdiction of Jefferson County, though, I had a feeling that wouldn't stop them from coming after us no matter who owned the property. There were over five thousand acres up there, so I was sure to find someplace to hide the manicure kit and book where the cops couldn't find them, assuming they didn't bring out the bloodhounds.

Fred was halfway on his way to the top of the hill when I caught up with him. Any other time I would have never caught up to him but he had stopped to sniff out something. When I got closer, I saw a dark hole under a rock ledge. Fred had found some critter's den. I was afraid he would run into it and wake a sleeping bear or mountain lion. I wanted to call him back, but didn't want to chance being heard by the deputies below. Sounds up here could travel for miles.

I walked over to Fred and whispered, "That's not a good place to hide the bag, old boy. The owner of that den might eat it for breakfast."

My fears were allayed when he didn't go into the den, and ran over to a rock pile several feet away. He looked at the rocks then looked back at me and barked. "Shh, Freddie," I whispered.

He barked again, so I rushed over to see what was so important before he did it again. He'd already started digging by the time I reached him. At first I thought he'd found another creature. I wasn't worried about snakes because I'd never come across one in the twenty years I lived up here. And I knew it couldn't be a large animal, so I assumed it was a marmot or chipmunk. It was neither. There was no hole, just a pile of rocks. Then it hit me. He had found the perfect hiding place. I could bury the plastic bag under the pile of rocks. Any bloodhounds should be distracted by what was hiding in the larger den. I looked at Fred in amazement. He sat there with a huge grin on his face. His dumb human finally caught on, or so I thought. Maybe I was imagining things; no dog is that smart.

The cops were gone by the time we'd finished hiding the evidence, and returned to my cabin. My fear that I was next to be searched turned out to be unfounded. The cops were nowhere in sight, so Fred and I went down to see if they had gone into Bonnie's house.

The flowerpot didn't look like it had been moved, for it was still covering the stain on her deck. Then I noticed a latch and padlock on the door. On closer examination, I saw where they had forced the door open, making it impossible to lock securely. At least they had the decency to jury rig a lock so no one could simply walk in. The key under the flowerpot would be of no help now, so all I could do was peek through the windows to confirm what I already knew. They had gone through her kitchen cabinets, and moved the living room furniture. I couldn't see into the bedroom, but could imagine the mattress on the floor, and all of her dresser drawers open. There was no longer any doubt in my mind that someone was trying to frame Bonnie by planting the copy of *Tom Sawyer*. I had a feeling once I checked into it, I'd find it belonged to Shelia.

I sneaked into Bonnie's hospital room early Saturday morning, and told her about the sheriff searching her home.

"Someone is trying to frame me?" she asked. I had guessed correctly that Margot would not be up this early, though, I didn't count on the head nurse at the nurses' station telling me to come back at visiting hours. I had pretended to leave, then came back from the hall on the other side of Bonnie's room, bypassing the nurses.

I held my finger to my lips in the universal sign to be quiet when she had asked the question too loudly. "It's the only logical explanation," I whispered. "Why else would they put the two things in your house that can tie you to Shelia's murder and then call the cops telling them where to find the evidence?"

"That sounds like my nail file, but are you sure it's her book?"

"She wrote 'Property of Shelia Clancy' on the inside cover."

Bonnie squirmed in an attempt to get comfortable and knocked a pillow on the floor. "Clancy? Oh, that must have been her maiden name. I wonder who's doing it. It can't be the kids or Appleton. They're all dead."

There was an extra pillow on the empty bed next to her, so I took it, and the one on the floor, and put them behind her head. "I'm pretty sure I know who the gray haired lady is, and you're not going to like it," I said once she'd settled back down.

"Oh, and who would that be?"

"I think you already know."

Bonnie reached for her water bottle and took a sip from the straw. "No, Jake, it's not Patty, if that's what you're thinking. She was with me the night Shelia was killed."

"I didn't say she killed anyone. I still think Craig did those dirty deeds. But she fits the description perfectly of the person who broke into your house to frame you."

She put the bottle back on the bedside table before answering. "It's not her, Jake."

I took a deep breath and held it for a minute. "Okay, Bon Bon, I really don't care anymore. I just need to get Julie's book and ring from whoever took them."

"What about Shelia's book? You're not going to leave it out in the weather are you?"

"It's wrapped up in the best plastic money can buy. I buried it in a grocery bag. Those bags are supposed to last a thousand years in the landfill, so it should be okay for a few days. I'll get it when I'm sure the cops aren't coming back."

I expected her to mention the nail file, too, but she caught me completely off guard. "I need you to do me a couple big favors, Jake."

"The last time you asked that I committed a crime hiding state's evidence. What kind of felony do you want me to commit this time?"

It was good to see her color had returned along with her smile. "Would you fix my front door for me?"

"Consider it done. What's the other favor?"

"Sneak me in some cigarettes. I'm going to die if I don't get one soon."

"I'll see what I can do," I lied. I had no intention of feeding her addiction. "Now tell me all you know about Patty."

"The gray haired woman wasn't Patty, Jake."

"How can you be so sure? I'd bet my next paycheck, if I ever get one, that it was her."

Bonnie started to laugh, but covered her mouth when she realized she might be heard by a nurse. "You can pay me with those cigarettes. Patty doesn't drive."

I was so sure it had been Patty who planted the evidence to frame Bonnie. Now I didn't have a clue who it was, but I knew I'd better find out before the woman I saw realized her frame didn't work.

This narrowed my list of suspects to one: Craig Renfield. I suppose he could have dressed up as an old lady to throw off anyone who had been watching Bonnie's. After all, I didn't get a close look at the old woman. Then again, he was way too tall. Stair handrails need to be between thirty-four and thirty-eight inches, according to most building codes, so the woman I saw had to be around five feet tall, give or take an inch. Whoever it was, I was sure she would try again, and I had the perfect plan to catch her.

CHAPTER SEVENTEEN

Removing the lock on Bonnie's door took all of five minutes with my portable grinder, and I had a new, pre-hung door installed in less than an hour. I used her old deadbolt so she wouldn't have to get new keys, however, I did remove the key from under the flowerpot and put it on my key chain where it would stay until she returned home. Working with my hands is the best way I know of to work out one's problems, or in my case, the perfect plan.

My original idea to install surveillance cameras went south when I saw online how much it would cost, so I came up with a low-tech solution that would make MacGyver proud. Bonnie had one of those lights that went on whenever someone came within proximity of its sensor. They have a photoelectric cell that prevents the light from coming on during the day, so I simply bypassed that feature by taping over it. Then I removed the bulb and replaced it with one of those adapters that have two power outlets and a bulb socket. After screwing her flood-light back in, I connected a long extension cord to one of the power outlets, and ran it up to my house where I plugged in a lamp and a radio. Now if anyone approached Bonnie's door, day or night, my lamp and radio would come on at the same time as Bonnie's floodlight.

To complete the system, I took an old camcorder I hadn't used in ten years and plugged its power adapter into the second outlet on Bonnie's modified security light. By turning the camcorder on and removing the battery, it would only record when something tripped the security light. The bottom of the camcorder was designed so it could be screwed into a tripod. I found a long bolt the same size and with the same thread pattern then drilled a hole in her top deck rail, inserted the bolt from the bottom, and attached the camcorder. A clear-plastic bag served to waterproof the contraption, and a rubber band around the lens kept that part of the plastic from distorting the picture. In the end, I had an alarm and surveillance system that would make Scrooge jealous.

Now that I was set to catch whoever had tried to frame Bonnie, I needed to get back to my problem. I didn't want to break into Appleton's cabin again, but I had to get Julie's property back.

By Monday morning, Fred and I were ready to visit Appleton's cabin and look for my property. This time I wasn't going to park my car anywhere near the scene of the crime where some nosy neighbor could get my license number. In one of my more inspired moments, I decided I would park a mile or two away, and ride my mountain bike the rest of the way. Poor Fred couldn't ride of course, so he was in for some overdue exercise. At least, that was the plan until I saw a Mercedes SUV come up my road. It had to be the author from the book signing, for although those rigs were not uncommon in the more affluent neighborhoods of Evergreen, their owners rarely ventured this far up a dirt road unless they were selling real estate.

"Mr. Martin, I hope you don't mind the intrusion, but I need your help," Wilson said when I went to meet him at his SUV. He was too scared to get out of the car.

I grabbed Fred by the collar in an attempt to make Wilson feel safer. "He won't bite unless you bite him first." He didn't even crack a smile, so I continued. "Why don't you come sit on my porch and tell me what I can do for you? I'd invite you in, but the house is a mess."

What I really didn't want him to see was my jury-rigged surveillance system. I hadn't planned on Bonnie's security light going on every time the wind blew the branches of a nearby aspen tree. Wilson might want to know why my lamp and radio kept going on and off. Then there was the telltale extension cord running out my back window, which might draw his attention to something not quite right.

Wilson didn't take his eyes off Fred as he cautiously got out of his SUV. "You sure he won't bite?"

"Hasn't bitten anyone in at least a week," I replied, while trying to count the freckles on the top of his head.

Wilson smiled nervously. It looked like he got my joke. "I've never been a dog person, you know. My mother was allergic to pet hair, so I never had any growing up."

"Wow! Not even a cat?"

"Not until after she passed, bless her soul." His head turned toward the sky and he crossed himself.

I picked up a stick, threw it as far as I could, and then let Fred go before Wilson could expand on his blessing. "Too bad, I'd be lost without Fred. He's the best friend I ever had. Shall we head to the porch before he comes back?"

"So what's on your mind? Don't tell me you're being sued?" I asked after we'd sat down on my porch chairs.

His pupils grew larger despite the bright sun. "How did you know?"

"That was the last thing you said to me the last time I saw you."

"Oh, right. Well, the parents of the girl are suing me for two million dollars. They say their daughter would have never gone into that mine if it hadn't been for my story. I heard rumors you suspect her and her boyfriend, what's his name, Cory something or other, might have been the ones who murdered the Marine. I'd be in your debt if you can help me prove it."

"Cory Weston, but who on earth told you I suspected them of murder?" I asked just as Fred came back with the stick and laid it at my feet.

Wilson failed to look at me when he answered. "I'd rather not say other than it's a good friend." His eyes never left my ferocious beast, a killer dog that couldn't so much as catch a squirrel.

He couldn't be that paranoid of dogs, so he was either extremely shy, or lying. "Right, the mysterious insider who works for the county. How do you expect me to help you, Paul, if you can't be honest with me?"

Wilson finally looked at me. "I could get into a lot of trouble if this gets out. You have to promise you won't repeat what I'm about to say."

I picked up Fred's stick and threw it again. Fred bolted off the porch, startling Wilson. "Mum's the word," I said, purposely avoiding any promise.

Wilson followed the stick with his eyes while shifting in his chair. He seemed to consider for a moment, before continuing without speaking to my face. "My friend works in the sheriff's office and has kept me up to date on the murders."

"Murders? You mean murder, don't you? Or is the sheriff not buying Appleton's suicide?"

He seemed relieved when Fred tired of the stick game and went off to chase Chatter. Wilson now gave me his full attention when he spoke. "My source tells me you don't believe Appleton killed himself, and you think those damn kids had something to do with it. So if you're correct, it is murders with an S."

Wilson was no longer playing defense, and knew it as he sat waiting for my response while stroking his goatee, and reading my face. Either he had been a psychologist at one time, or spent enough time with one, for it made me consider telling him everything I knew and suspected, but something made me hold back. It was like when a telemarketer calls unannounced and starts asking personal questions. I didn't know this guy except from the book signing, and I didn't feel comfortable.

"I don't remember saying that to the Jeffco deputy. Your source must have got it from Deputy White over in Park County. Is that where your friend works?"

"No, she works in Golden. I can only guess that White and Jeffco are sharing info on the case. White must have reported your suspicions. So it's true then?"

"So it is written, so it shall be," I replied.

Wilson cracked a small smile. "You mean 'So it shall be written. So it shall be done.' don't you? *The Ten Commandments* has got to be one of my favorite movies of all time."

"Is that where I heard it? Sorry, I'm not as old as you. I think I've only seen that movie once or twice on television when I was a kid, but you got my point. If Appleton killed himself, then Moses loved BLT sandwiches."

Wilson had to laugh. "You have a way with words, Jake. Have you ever considered writing as a career? I'll have to tell my Jewish friends that one."

I couldn't decide whether to thank him or say something sarcastic. Doesn't this guy know I am a writer?

Fred had returned without his stick or squirrel and lay down by my feet. Wilson didn't seem as bothered by Fred as he was before. "So will you help me, Jake? I can pay you for your time."

The mention of pay not only got my attention, it got Fred's, too. He raised his head and stared at Wilson. It must have been the pleading in Wilson's voice.

"I'd like to help you, Paul, but I'm a little busy at the moment." I didn't bother to confide I'd be busy committing another felony.

"Besides the money, which would be substantial, you might also recover that book Appleton stole from you."

"My copy of *Tom Sawyer*? You think those kids had it?"

He knew he had me hooked, I could see it in his Hannibal Lecter smile. "According to my source,

Cory's backpack is still in the cave, and I think you will find both our books in it. That's what I want you to get."

"Hold on, pilgrim. Unless I'm losing all my marbles, you were asking me if White mentioned finding anything in the backpack the last time you were here. Now you're telling me it's still in the mine?"

"That was before my friend told me it wasn't recovered. He only knew it existed." His response was too quick for it to be a lie.

"How would your source know that?" I asked, noting that he was no longer salivating over the thought of fresh meat now that Fred was watching him. "I mean, wouldn't the rescue team, or whoever pulled the kids out of the mine, have retrieved the backpack too?"

"The backpack wasn't with the kids. It fell to a lower level. The mine shaft has several levels that were built out of wood and the wood rotted out years ago, making it too dangerous for the rescue team to go after the backpack."

"But it's not too dangerous for me?"

Wilson let out a short laugh that sounded more like a snort. "It's the bureaucracy. They're so afraid of OSHA and a thousand other rules, they couldn't go after it without somebody higher up signing off, and that might take weeks. I'm sure someone as fit as you would have no trouble climbing down there on a rope and get the backpack before they do."

He had trouble looking me in the eyes again, which made me wonder how much of his story was pure fiction. "Well, I suppose it won't hurt to check it out."

Wilson did all the talking after I accepted his retainer and told him what he needed to know about Cory and Jennifer, leaving out incriminating details like how Fred found Bonnie's manicure kit in the kids' trash, and the bloody shirt from Appleton's cabin.

The five hundred dollar check he gave me would go a long way to catching up my bills and buying dog food. But little did he know I would have gone after the backpack anyway. He had no idea how much Julie's copy of Tom Sawyer meant to me, so when he told me he wanted me to go back to the mine where the kids fell to their death, I didn't argue. I did ask what was in the backpack besides books, but all he would say was it would prove he had nothing to do with the kids' death.

Wilson finally left around noon, making it too late to head for Mosquito Pass. As badly as I wanted to get going, I also needed to put Wilson's check in the bank before he changed his mind. We would start out early the next morning now that I no longer had to search Appleton's cabin, but that plan would change later that night when my homemade alarm stopped working.

It was the silence that woke me at two in the morning. I had become used to the radio going on and off every few minutes, and fallen sound asleep, but woke with a start when my subconscious told me something was wrong. I went out to the kitchen where I had placed the radio, and saw the headlights of a car backing out of Bonnie's drive.

With shotgun in hand, and attack dog at my side, I crept down to Bonnie's house. I went up her back stairs while Fred ran around to the front. I knew the intruder was gone, so I didn't worry about Fred not being armed. He probably knew it too, for he didn't so much as growl on our trip down the hill.

I tried shining my flashlight into Bonnie's kitchen, just to make sure we were alone, before joining Fred on the front porch. He was sniffing at the deck rail, where I had placed my camcorder, and turned to bark at me when he saw me. I couldn't see much in the moonless night, but soon discovered why he greeted me that way. My camcorder was gone. Further investigation showed the extension cord had been unplugged, and Bonnie's flower pot had been moved again.

We spent the next thirty minutes checking Bonnie's house before locking everything up and heading home. Nothing was out of place and I didn't see anything that wasn't supposed to be there, so we went on home after plugging the extension cord back in. I could hear my radio immediately, and realized that must have been what alerted the would-be burglar.

"And he took your camcorder?" Bonnie asked when I called her to tell her about the failed burglary. She was staying with Margot in Cherry Creek since being released from the hospital, and had called me several times to ask about my progress, but each time I had nothing new to report—until now.

"If it *is* a he," I answered. "Maybe it's the gray haired lady again. We'll never know now, will we? I wish I wasn't so cheap and had bought a real surveillance system."

"It's not Patty, Jake."

If only I could see her face, I'd know for sure if she was mad or joking. "I know, Bon, you already told me. Patty doesn't drive."

"Too bad he took your camcorder. Then we would know for sure."

"Well, whoever it was, he or she is going to be in for a real shock next time they come snooping," I wished she could see my face. I had just thought of a way to get even, and the expression on my face must have made me look like Batman's Joker.

The pause on Bonnie's end told me she didn't understand. "I mean that literally, Bon, so don't touch the doorknob until I deactivate my little surprise."

"What?" she asked.

"I'm going to wire your door to the household current. Whoever touches it will be knocked flat."

"Please don't do that, Jake. It would be my luck the perpetrator will die of a heart attack and his family will sue me for everything I've got." She did have a point; there were far too many instances lately where homeowners got in trouble for protecting their property.

In the end, I was able to reset my Rube Goldberg surveillance system with a camcorder Bonnie had that was even older than mine. This time I used my twenty-foot extension ladder to put the camera in a tree where it couldn't be removed unless the intruder happened to be the offspring of Big Foot, or have a ladder of his own. I also hid the extension cord in the gutter so it wasn't so obvious.

With my ladder locked up in my tool shed, Fred and I were finally on our way to Mosquito Pass.

By the time we passed Pine Junction, I knew we were not alone.

CHAPTER EIGHTEEN

This time I didn't stop at the service station in Fairplay. I didn't need the nosy owner calling his brother-in-law, Deputy White, to alert him of my presence. But I did need to check out who was following us, so I waited until I passed the station before pulling over to the side of the road.

My paranoia told me it was Craig Renfield. The car had been too far away to tell for sure, but I was pretty sure it was his beat-up Toyota. The driver pulled into the gas station but didn't get out to pump gas. He must have been surprised when White's brother-in-law came out to do it for him. I wasted no time in getting back on the road before he could follow us again.

I seemed to have lost the car by the time I turned onto Mosquito Gulch Road. Not that it would matter; the old Toyota couldn't possibly make it up the pass.

Several ATVs and dirt bikes raced by me belching blue smoke from their two-cycle motors and spraying my windshield with rocks and dirt as I approached the spot where Bonnie and I had parked the last time we were here. There was some kind of off-road rally going on, or school must have let out for summer vacation. Either way, it was impossible to park on the road because of the traffic, so I put the old Wagoneer in four-wheel drive and left the road, heading for the mine.

Nobody seemed to notice our ascent up the side of the hill, for no one bothered to follow us. Perhaps the slope was too steep for them, but more likely they couldn't see me past the clouds of dust they were creating.

The ground leveled off into what was once a mule trail just below the mine where a huge pile of tailings was created by some poor soul who had dug it out so many years ago. From there the trail went up the hill another hundred feet or so by cutting switchbacks into the side of the mountain until it wound its way to the top of the tailings. It was far too steep and narrow for my Jeep, so I parked, and would have to walk the rest of the way. Fred was out of the Jeep and sniffing the ground the minute I opened the door. The scent led him up the trail and out of my sight.

He couldn't know the floor inside the mine had collapsed, sending Cory and Jennifer to their deaths. I didn't want the same thing happening to my best friend, and ran after him.

I was gasping for air when I made it to the top, but found the breath to call him. "Fred! Get back here this instant."

His head poked out of a dark hole in the side of the mountain.

"Come here, boy," I pleaded, bending down to his level. To my relief, he ran toward me, and planted a big, wet kiss on my face.

"Can you be a good boy and stay out here while I check on that mine?" I asked, once I wiped off my face.

Fred sat on his haunches and barked. "Good, boy. Now, stay," I said, and headed toward the entrance.

The yellow police tape stretched across the opening didn't stop me; I was just glad it couldn't be seen from the road where someone might see me breaking the law. I turned on my flashlight, stepped inside, and crept toward what used to be an old wood floor. Now it was just a hole in the ground with slivers of decaying wood around the perimeter that resembled rotten teeth waiting to devour their next victim. It looked like the mouth of the three-headed dog guarding the gates of Hell I had seen in a Greek Mythology class. I was trying to recall the creature's name when Fred came up behind me, nearly making me drop my flashlight.

"Didn't I tell you to stay outside?" I asked, grasping my chest. "Do I need to tie you to the Jeep?"

Fred barked, ran back toward the entrance, then turned around to look at me, and barked again. The hair along his spine looked like porcupine quills.

I hurried back to the entrance and grabbed his collar when he started to growl. "What is it, boy? Is someone out there?"

Fred acted like he'd seen a Yeti and wanted to eat him for lunch. I couldn't see any snowmen or anyone else, so I went to the edge of the tailing pile for a better look. I began to wish I'd brought binoculars. Maybe Fred could see something I couldn't. The four-wheelers had moved on, along with their dust, but there was someone parked on the road. A chill ran up my spine when I thought I recognized the car that had been following us earlier. It had to be my overactive imagination, for I knew there was no way a two-wheel-drive sedan with only inches of ground clearance could have come this far. It was probably a vehicle belonging to one of the off-roaders or some hikers. I finally convinced myself that was what Fred must have heard, and went back to the mine.

For some stupid reason, the name Cerberus popped into my head when I saw the splintered floor again. It was the name of the dog guarding Hades I couldn't remember earlier. The shaft consisted of a series of platforms with a ladder between each level. The rescue workers didn't risk the danger of going below the level where they found the kids. It was a wonder the second platform didn't collapse from the impact of their fall.

Paul Wilson said the pack had fallen to a lower level. Only a fool would have gone any further, and while I never claimed to be a genius, I had a trump card most fools didn't. My Jeep had a winch with two hundred feet of cable I could use to lower myself into the pit. There was no question in my mind about retrieving the backpack. All I had to do was get the Jeep up to the mine without killing myself.

I let Fred play sentry, watching for Yeti, while I climbed back down to my Jeep and prepared to climb the pile of tailings. Going up the mule trail was out of the question because of the narrow switchbacks. The Jeep could never make those turns without tumbling sideways. The only option was to make it climb straight up the tailing pile and over the top. The ancient Jeep had manual lock-out hubs and a little switch in the glove compartment that would make all four wheels spin when needed. Unlike modern four-by-fours, where only one wheel per axle worked, the old Quadra-track's used all their wheels.

No sooner had I started my ascent than I felt the Jeep going sideways. I began to wish I had used the winch to pull it to the top instead, but it was too late. Rocks and gravel were flying everywhere, and I was within seconds of the Jeep rolling down the hill and squashing me like the bug this place was named for.

My first instinct was to let up on the gas, but I knew that would be suicide, so I turned the wheel in the opposite direction of the slide, and floored the gas pedal. The tires bit into the gravel and propelled the Jeep to the top, like I knew what I was doing. Fred was a lot smarter than his master and had stayed behind to watch the show from a safe distance.

All of a sudden I heard hooting, horns, and whistling. The off-road riders had returned and stopped to watch the idiot in his old Jeep try to kill himself. The last thing I needed now was for one of them to leave the road and come up to join us. I didn't worry about another four-wheeler trying it, but motorcycles were something else. I knew if we stayed here, it would be only minutes before one of the dirt-bike riders came to see if we needed help, so I summoned Fred into the Jeep, and pretended to leave.

The mule trail lead away from the mine and on toward Leadville, so I put the Jeep back into regular four-wheel drive, and acted like climbing the tailing had simply been to gain access to the trail. I didn't have to go far before we were out of sight from the riders below where I stopped the Jeep and waited.

Fred jumped out and ran over to some rocks. The trail had been cut through an ancient landslide and there were rocks and boulders on both sides of it. I saw a creature scoot from under one pile and run for cover under another. It looked like a marmot, but

Fred must have thought it was Chatter. I was so intent on watching the show that I nearly jumped out of my skin when my cell phone went off.

"Jake?" It was a voice I knew well.

"Bonnie! How are you?"

"Where have you been, Jake? I've been trying to get you all day."

"I'm up on Mosquito Pass. Reception up here is pretty bad. I'm surprised you got me now."

"What are you doing up there?"

"Enjoying the view while Fred chases Chatter's cousin. You should see it, Bon. I found a little mule trail that must have been cut into the mountain by whoever dug the mine. I can see all the way to Leadville from here."

"Are you crazy, Jake? Two people already lost their lives in there. Please don't make it three."

"It's already three, don't forget Drake. He was the first."

When she didn't respond quickly enough, I knew without the benefit of seeing her face that she didn't like my wise-aleck reply. "Sorry, Bon Bon. I appreciate your concern, but Wilson thinks the kids had Julie's copy of Tom Sawyer and I've got to get it back."

"Please don't go in there, Jake."

"It okay, I'll lower myself with my winch so there's no danger of falling. Now tell me why you called. Are you okay?"

"I called to see if you wouldn't mind coming to get me. Margot is driving me crazy. She won't let me smoke, and doesn't have a drop of booze anywhere."

I laughed. "Is she there, Bon? I'd like to talk to her."

Bonnie hesitated. Was I that transparent? "She's not my mother, Jake. You don't need her permission."

"Sorry, Bon."

"For your information, I've never felt better. The physical therapist can come to my home in Evergreen, just as she does here. I've already ordered a treadmill. All you have to do is pick it up for me on the way home."

"Okay, Bon. Is tomorrow morning okay? Wherever you bought the treadmill will be closed by the time I get there tonight." I knew Margot wouldn't let her leave if she wasn't all right.

"Tomorrow is fine if you promise not to go in that mine until I'm there. Otherwise, I'm calling Deputy White and tell him you're up there."

"You win, Bon. It's getting too dark anyway. See you first thing tomorrow." I didn't like lying to her, but the last thing I needed right then was to have White know I was up there.

The sun was setting behind the snow-covered mountains on the west side of Leadville by the time I got off the phone with Bonnie. If memory served me right, those were Colorado's two tallest peaks: Mount

Elbert and Mount Massive. It would be dark soon and I needed to get back to work, but I had to capture the moment by taking a picture with my cell phone. The sun was moving so fast on the city below, it looked like one of those time-lapse movies on TV.

"Stand there a minute, Fred, so I can get your picture," I said when he came running back.

He stopped long enough for me to capture a shot I was sure would go viral on YouTube. He could have been the poster boy for *Bark* magazine. His head was blocking out the sun, making it look like he had a halo.

The off-roaders and the mystery car were gone from the road below when we got back to the mine, reminding me of what little time I had before it got too dark to see, so I positioned the Jeep as close to the mine as I could and started playing out the cable. The surface there was flat and level. The only obstruction was the remains of tracks from an old ore cart that must have been used to haul debris from the mine, creating the pile of tailings I drove up earlier.

"Stay here and let me know if we get any visitors, Fred," I said as I lowered myself down the shaft. I had thought about locking him in the Jeep, but knew my cell phone would be worthless inside the mine. He was all I had to go get help if something went wrong.

The cable slowly lowered me to where Cory and Jennifer had fallen to their deaths. It made me sad when I thought of her poetry, and the love she showed for her unborn child. I stopped long enough to say a prayer, and waited until there was enough slack to allow me some movement before pushing the stop button on the winch's remote. I wasn't foolish enough to let go of my lifeline. The light from above had disappeared once the sun had set behind Mount Elbert, and it was still too early for the moon to shine its feeble beam into the mine. I turned on my flashlight and prayed the battery didn't quit on me.

I made a quick scan of my surroundings then shined the light on the platform below, and saw the backpack. With one more look above and a couple Hail Marys, I crept over the side of the entrance to Hades. Fred was watching me from above, and the reflection I saw in his eyes reminded me once more of Cerberus guarding the gates of Hell. I removed the slack from the cable, and pushed the button to lower me down.

I was less than four feet from the backpack when my flashlight went dead. Then the winch jammed. Was someone up there? No, Fred would have barked if there was. It had to be Murphy and the luck of the Irish. I had wound the cable around my waist and secured my foot in a small loop at the bottom where a hook was attached to the end of the cable. I let the cable spin me around, freeing me from its grasp, and then pulled myself up enough to free my foot before lowering myself to the floor below. Still holding on to my lifeline, I tentatively put my weight on the platform, testing to see if it would collapse on me like the floor above had on the kids. It seemed to be solid enough to hold my two hundred pounds.

With one hand free of the cable, I smacked the flashlight against my thigh and said another prayer. I really wanted to swear, but knew my guardian angel might take offense. She must have liked what she heard, for the flashlight flickered back to life.

The backpack was within reach so I grabbed it, put its straps around my arms, and started climbing up the cable. The cable wasn't much different than the rope we had been required to climb so many years ago in gym class. I hadn't forgotten how to use my feet, hands, and arms to slowly inch my way to the top. But it was much thinner than those old ropes, which made it far more difficult to climb. Nor did those old ropes hurt nearly as badly as the wire fibers that cut into my hands when I grasped a frayed strand.

I finally emerged from the dark pit with bloody hands and more fatigued than if I had run a marathon. The altitude and the extra weight I'd put on lately had taken its toll. I was exhausted. All I wanted to do was lie down to catch my breath, but something was wrong. Fred should have been there waiting for me. I had been holding the flashlight in my mouth, so I grasped it with my right hand, because of the metal slivers in my left, and scanned my surroundings, looking for my dog. Then everything went dark.

CHAPTER NINETEEN

Julie was wiping my forehead with a wet cloth and kissing me at the same time. "Wake up, Jake, or you'll freeze up here. Please, honey, please wake up."

I slowly opened my eyes, "Julie! Is it really you?"

She barked then wiped my face some more.

"Fred!" I shouted when I started to come to. "Where's Julie?" Then I realized I'd been dreaming, and felt a terrible pain in my arm and the back of my head.

I sat up and reached for Fred, but yelled when the pain shot down my arm from the shoulder. Fred backed away for a moment then came back with his tail between his legs.

"What happened, boy? God, I wish you could talk. Did you get hit too?" I looked around to see if we were alone. I couldn't have been unconscious for long, for it was still dark with no hint of a rising sun shining its light into the mine. If not for my flashlight still burning, we would have been in total darkness.

Holding my sore shoulder with my right hand, I reached for the light with my left. It only seemed to hurt if I lifted my arm too high, which I did, and yelled again. Actually, it was more of a whimper because I didn't scare Fred this time. "Can you get the flashlight, Freddie?"

He barked then licked me some more. It had been worth a try even though I really didn't think he'd understand. Then it hit me why my arm was hurting. The backpack was gone. Whoever took it must have torn the straps off my arms and nearly taken my arm with it. That narrowed it down to someone quite strong, so I could rule out the little old lady who broke into Bonnie's.

Fred wasn't going to get the flashlight for me and it wasn't going to come to me no matter how much I pleaded, so I reached out for it with my good arm. To my surprise, Fred went over and picked it up before I could. I'm sure he thought it was some kind of stick.

"Good, boy," I said when he brought it back to me. I reached out to rub his neck before taking the flashlight from him and felt something sticky.

"What's this, Freddie?" I asked, shining the light on his neck. His entire neck and face were covered with an oily orange substance.

Fred let out a cry and backed away from me when I shined the light in his eyes. "It's okay, Freddie," I said ever so softly after noticing his eyes were red and puffy. "You know I wouldn't hurt you for the world."

He looked at me with the saddest eyes I've seen outside a seal exhibit.

I went back to my examination of Fred then realized why my eyes were watering. No wonder he didn't sound the alarm before I was knocked out; someone had pepper sprayed him.

Bonnie wasn't the least bit upset when I called her early Wednesday morning to tell her we would be late picking her up from her sister's. "It's okay, Jake. Margot is taking me shopping at the Cherry Creek Mall, and I was going to call you anyway." She didn't ask why I would be late and I didn't offer an excuse.

"Why don't you wait a couple days before coming to get me? We're going to the Botanic Gardens tomorrow and maybe the museum. I'd forgotten how much there is to do down here. Oh, I almost forgot. Could I ask you for a big favor?"

"Sure, Bon." I tried not to sound too relieved.

"Would you mind picking up my mail for me? Margot's been telling me how I shouldn't leave it sitting out on the road because anyone can steal my identity now-a-days." She was referring to how our mailboxes were half a mile from our homes, stuck down on Upper Bear Creek Road, where anyone could help themselves.

"No problem, Bon. Just call me when you're ready to come home." I knew it might be sooner than later for it was a rare week when she and Margot didn't end up fighting about something. But it should be enough time, without Bonnie tagging along, for me to find Craig Renfield and make him pay for nearly breaking my arm and pepper spraying my dog. It didn't take a PI license to know who owned the old Toyota up on Mosquito Pass.

This time I didn't park in Casa Bonita's lot, and drove straight to Renfield's house on Saulsbury. Like Cory and Jennifer's house two doors down, it had seen better days. I could see several shingles missing and the paint on its clapboard siding was faded and peeling. Several of the single-pane windows were broken and their screens ripped so they looked like miniature flags flapping in the wind.

Fred followed me to the front door where I had to knock because the doorbell button was hanging by a single wire, and clearly not working. I could feel my rage building and, fantasized about blowing his head off with my shotgun. That wasn't going to happen because I didn't bring it, but I quickly improvised and imagined myself punching him in the face then knocking him to the ground where I'd stomp on his head until he stopped breathing. He had to be fifty pounds lighter and four inches shorter than me, so I'm sure I'd come out ahead if this didn't go well, even though I was ten years older.

"Well, if it isn't Timmy and Lassie. What are you two doing here?" Craig asked when he answered his door, holding a baseball bat in his hand.

I checked my anger at the site of his weapon. "Do you mind telling me where you were yesterday?"

"I asked first," he said. His upper lip rose a couple millimeters. I'd seen Fred do the same before going after Chatter.

His remark caught me off guard. I hadn't heard a response like that since grade school. We lost eye contact when I saw movement in his kitchen. "Someone hit me over the head and pepper sprayed my dog yesterday," I said, looking past him into the house. "Someone driving a beat-up Toyota like yours."

His lip uncurled into a slight smile. "I traded that piece of junk off last week," he said, nodding in the direction of his driveway. A late model SUV was parked in a detached garage at the back of his lot.

"What happen? You lose a muffler on Mosquito Pass?"

His smirk disappeared faster than my last paycheck. "You're a real smartass, aren't you?" he said, and shut the door in my face.

If not for Fred yelping when I pulled too tightly on his collar, I might have kicked in Craig's door. I hadn't been this upset since Junior High when the class bully pulled down my gym shorts in front of a cute cheerleader. Fred left my side when I let him go, and ran back toward the Jeep. I quickly followed him for fear he might run into the street.

"You did that on purpose, didn't you, Freddie?" He was sitting on his haunches next to my Jeep when I caught up to him.

He didn't answer, of course, but he did smile as we drove away.

I called Paul Wilson as soon as we got home. It was a call I should have made sooner, but I had been too mad to think clearly. Now that I realized it probably wasn't Craig's Toyota I had seen on the pass, I needed to face up to the fact that I'd have to give Wilson his money back. He seemed to be one of those people who never answer, so I left a message to call me back, and went to bed.

I couldn't sleep, thinking of the incident on the pass while watching the minutes flip by on my alarm clock like the scores of a baseball game in an old movie. The clock was a relic from the seventies, the kind where the numbers were printed on four mechanical wheels that turned when the time changed. If it wasn't Craig's Toyota I had seen, then who was it that stole the backpack, and why? Why did they wait for me to retrieve it instead of going after it themselves? All four wheels where turning to display the number ten when Wilson returned my call.

"You're telling me you found the backpack, and then someone hit you over the head, and nearly broke your arm taking it from you?" He sounded very upset, so I expected he'd want his money back.

"Right after pepper spraying my dog."

"Pepper spray?"

"I think so. I've been doing some research while waiting for your call, and it seems anyone can buy that stuff."

"Is he okay?"

"Yeah, he's okay now. I gave him a good bath when we got home, but I doubt if he'll ever eat scrambled eggs with hot sauce again."

I cleared my throat before asking the next question. "How well do you know Craig Renfield?"

"Not at all, why?"

"I thought I saw his car up there just before I was knocked out. He says he traded it off last week, but I only have his word for that, so he's still my number one suspect. What I can't fathom is why he wanted the backpack so badly, and for that matter, how he knew it was there."

Wilson didn't answer. I was beginning to think he didn't realize I had asked a question and was ready to speak again when he beat me to it. "Well, I did tell him I would be willing to pay dearly for his copy of *Tom Sawyer* if he ever recovered it."

"I thought you said you didn't know him."

"I don't. It was at the signing when I asked him. I told him I'd pay a nice finder's fee if he could get the kids to sell me theirs." Then he paused again. I was beginning to realize he was the kind to choose his words carefully. "You've got to get that backpack from him, Jake. I'll pay whatever you ask."

"What is in there, Paul?"

"Why don't you meet me at that pizza place down the road from you, say tomorrow at noon, and I'll fill you in?"

Wilson hung up before I could object.

CHAPTER TWENTY

Paul Wilson was late for our meeting at Beau Jo's, so I let Fred out of my Jeep to chase sticks in the creek behind the parking lot. Except for takeout, I hadn't been to any of the Beau Jo's restaurants since Julie died. They reminded me too much of the day I fell for her, when we had eaten at the one in Idaho Springs after window shopping with Fred. She had thought it was so cute the way he held his own leash while following us. I often wondered who she loved more, me or Fred.

We didn't have to wait long before I saw Wilson's Mercedes SUV pull into the parking lot. Fred dropped his stick at my feet and began to growl. "You really don't like him very much, do you, Freddie?" He never once took his eyes off the SUV while I escorted him back to the Jeep.

Wilson must not have seen us for he headed straight for the restaurant after getting out of his car. I ruffled the fur on Fred's head and asked him to behave himself before locking him in the Jeep and running to catch Wilson. "Wait up, Paul," I yelled.

He stopped short of entering the restaurant, giving me the chance to catch up with him. "Jake! I didn't see you over there. Sorry, I'm late."

"No problem. Fred needed some exercise anyway. I got up too late to take him on our walk around the lake, but he had fun chasing ducks and sticks in the creek."

Wilson glanced over at my Jeep where Fred had his big head sticking out the half-open window. "Looks like he recovered from the pepper spray," he said, and then turned to go inside.

We had taken a table overlooking the creek where I had been watching a small brood of ducklings follow their mother in the water while Wilson studied the menu. "By the way, Jake, how's that arm?"

"It's almost back to normal, thanks for asking."

"Well, if you need to, get it looked at, and send me the bill."

"Wow, thanks, Paul, but I don't think that'll be necessary. It should be as good as new in a day or two." I didn't mention the reason I hadn't seen the doctor is because I didn't have insurance. I was still paying for the last time I went to the ER. I'd sworn I'd die before going back again, after getting the bill.

His eyes went back to the menu. "Beautizers instead of appetizers, that's cute. Have you tried the stuffed mushrooms? They sure sound good."

"No, I usually order one of their mountain pie pizzas. There's no way I can finish one of those, much less an appetizer." I didn't mention my regular order of a whole pizza was so I'd have leftovers for Fred.

It was obvious Wilson had been making small talk, for he didn't so much as grunt a response, and kept his nose buried in the menu. I wondered how to cut to the chase, and ask about the backpack when the waitress saved me.

"Would you gentlemen care for anything to drink?" she asked.

Wilson looked up from his menu, and hooked his thumbs in his suspenders. "Can I get a Fat Tire, gorgeous?"

She blushed before turning to me. "And you, sir?"

I felt bad for her. I knew she went to Bonnie's church and couldn't be more than a couple years out of high school. Wilson had to be pushing sixty. "Just black coffee, please," I answered, handing her my menu. "And I'll take one of the Classic Calzones specials when you get a chance." I wasn't sure who was paying, and Fred needed to cut back on people food anyway.

"How about you, Sir?" she asked Wilson, without looking up from her order pad. "Are you ready to order, too?"

He pulled on one of his suspender straps and let it snap back into place before stroking his goatee. His eyes were all over her. "As much as I'd love to have one of your mountain pies, I've got to stay in shape, so how about a Caesar salad with lots of grated cheese on top."

I'll bet it was all the waitress could do to not laugh in his face. Even I knew the suspenders were probably because there wasn't a belt made that could fit his waist.

"So tell me, Paul, what's in the backpack anyway?" I asked after the waitress left.

He looked around at the other tables before answering. "I like the way you come right to the point, Jake. As a writer, I do have a tendency to beat around the bush."

"And?" I wanted to say something about how good writers didn't use clichés, but let it go.

Wilson removed his glasses and looked directly at me. "First you have to promise that whatever I tell you stays in this room."

"Seems I've heard that one before. Have you been to Vegas lately?"

He didn't get my joke, and continued staring at me without blinking.

"Mum's the word, scout's honor, and all that. Now, you want to tell me what's in that backpack that has you so riled up?"

He smiled. It wasn't a friendly smile, but one I'd expect Freddie Krueger to flash at me just before he slashed my throat. "Okay, I wasn't completely honest when I told you I made up the story of lost treasure. And if my guess is right those kids beat me to it."

"Are you telling me there's gold in that backpack?"

"Worth at least a hundred grand, maybe more depending on the condition and rarity of the coins," he answered quickly. His voice was so low, I could barely hear him over the background noise of the restaurant.

I whistled, causing several people to look up from their meal. "But if they did find the treasure, I fail to see how their parents can sue you."

Wilson leaned in closer, I assumed to keep anyone else from hearing, "I also didn't tell you someone broke into my place just before the kids went missing, and stole all my notes."

His breath smelled of cigarettes, so I scooted back from the table before speaking. "You didn't have copies or a backup?"

He seemed to forget our audience and raised his voice. "They got that, too. They took my flash drive with all my notes, but that's not the point. With my notes and the right copy of *Tom Sawyer*, they had everything they needed to find the treasure."

"So you didn't decode the riddle then."

He looked annoyed. "Of course not. Why else would I be searching for copies of the book?"

I thought about asking him if his notes were printed on a dot-matrix printer, but let it go. There was no sense letting him know I had found his notes at Appleton's. "So those kids had the key-copy of *Tom Sawyer* after all, and once they stole your notes, all they had to do was go up to Mosquito Pass and retrieve the gold."

"You catch on quick, Jake, but I couldn't care less about the coins. It's my notes that will hang me. If the parents discover it was because of me that those two fell to their deaths, I could lose everything. If you get my notes back, you can keep the coins."

"And how am I supposed to do that? The only suspect I can think of claims he traded off his car last week. I have no idea where to look, even if I wanted to."

Wilson gave me his Freddie Kruger smile again. "Oh, I think you will want to find it. The book the kids used to crack the code was yours."

"How do you know that?"

He held his index finger to his lips. "Hold it down, please."

I took a deep breath, and subconsciously began counting to ten, but only got to eight before he interrupted. "I'm not at liberty to say, but my source told me the kids got the book from Appleton."

"It would help me believe you if I knew who your source is," I said, while staring him in the eyes, knowing if he was lying he would turn away. He didn't.

"A little birdie told me, Jake." The smile was back. "And finding it won't be hard at all. That same birdie tells me your buddy, Craig Renfield, has it. He didn't trade off the Toyota until *after* he took the backpack."

He stopped talking when the waitress returned with our drinks. It was all the time I needed to end the meeting before I lost it.

"Could you put my meal in a doggy bag, miss?" I asked the waitress. I knew Wilson had lied about talking to Craig at the book signing, because Craig had left before Wilson could speak to him. He also lied about the coins, for he said it was gold ore at the signing. But something told me he wasn't lying about Julie's book, which made me want to grab him by the throat and make him tell the truth.

Wilson waited once again for the waitress to leave before continuing. "Is that a no, Jake? Are you really going to pass on the chance of making a hundred grand for a few minutes work?"

"No, Paul, I'll get the backpack, and it's not because of the coins, if they exist."

Fred would have to eat dog food tonight; I didn't wait for my calzone.

CHAPTER TWENTY-ONE

I spent the next two days trying to finish my latest eBook. I was stuck after finishing the chapter on proper attic ventilation. Long before computers and word processors, writers in my situation would succumb to almost anything to avoid writing. Pencil sharpening was probably the most common, so I performed the modern ritual of that task by convincing myself I was researching when in fact I was only wasting time on social media, and taking long walks with Fred. The problem of how to find the backpack never left my subconscious. By Saturday, Bonnie was ready to come home.

"If she wasn't my twin sister, I'd swear I had been adopted," Bonnie said as I turned onto Sixth Avenue heading for the hills. She had been complaining, ever since Fred and I picked her up, about how Margot had treated her. At least I didn't have to stop to pick up the treadmill, because they had called her earlier to say it was on back order.

She just finished telling me she hadn't had a cigarette in a week when she noticed me rubbing my upper arm. "Something wrong, Jake? I've noticed you have a terrible look on your face every time you touch that arm."

"Just a little bruise. I'm sure it's nothing compared to the way Fred must be feeling."

"Fred? What's wrong with Fred?" she asked, turning to look at him.

"Someone sprayed him with pepper spray."

Her mouth opened wider than any dentist could hope for. "Pepper spray! Why would someone do that?"

I proceeded to tell her about our little trip back to Mosquito Pass from the time Wilson gave me the five hundred dollar retainer up to when I woke up with Fred licking my face, and the orange stain on his neck.

"Oh you poor boy, Freddie," she said, petting him on the head. Then, turning to me, she asked. "Is he okay?"

"Yeah, he's fine now. I gave him a good scrubbing when we got home. I think the bath hurt him more than the spray. You would think a water-dog would love it, but I swear he thought I was punishing him."

She cut in when I stopped talking long enough to concentrate on merging onto I-70. "Who could have done such a thing?"

"The only one I can think of is Craig Renfield, but then, it's not his style. He's more of the 'shoot them with a real gun' person."

Bonnie turned around to face Fred. "I wish you could talk, Freddie, and tell Aunt Bonnie who did that to you. I'd beat them up for you."

"He's not telling, Bon, and you're in no shape to be beating up anyone. Didn't your doctor's say to get some rest?"

"Can you believe those jerks? Lay off the booze, no smoking and walk on the stupid treadmill twice a day. I might as well be dead."

We drove another five or ten minutes in silence. Fred had lain back down on the rear seat, and Bonnie was now staring out her window at the traffic on US 40, which ran adjacent to the freeway. My mind was still trying to answer her first question of who could have sprayed Fred. "It was either a woman or someone afraid of dogs, or maybe both."

It was enough to break her trance, and she turned from her window. "Why would you make a remark like that? I've never known you to be sexist."

"I'm not bashing women, Bonnie. In fact, I had ruled out a woman because of how the backpack was torn from my arm, but then that *would* be sexist, wouldn't it? I'm trying to think of who would be the most likely to carry pepper spray."

She didn't look angry, just curious, with her right brow raised half an inch higher than the left. "And a guy is too macho to carry pepper spray? You men, you're all the same."

"Sorry, Bon. I guess it could have been a man, maybe a mailman. I mean, who else would have one of those things?"

"Joggers, hikers, and even cops carry them."

It was my turn to stare in awe. "Cops?"

"You should watch the show sometime. You might learn something."

It took a second to realize she was referring to the TV show called Cops. "I better get you home, *muy pronto*. The lack of booze is making you meaner than a pit bull."

Her smirk disappeared into a frown. "Oh, I'm so sorry, Jake, I didn't mean to hurt your feelings. I'm so used to fighting with Margot. Please forgive me."

"I'm the one who should be sorry, Bon. It was foolish of me to think only a woman would carry pepper spray."

She smiled, and turned back to her window. "I wonder what's in the backpack."

"Wilson claims there's over a hundred thousand in gold coins and Julie's book. Says he doesn't care about the money and I can have it. He just wants his notes back so the kids' parents don't sue him."

"What?" she asked, no longer looking out at the distant mountains

"That's what he said. He didn't mention the book until he saw that the coins were the wrong bait to make me bite."

I could almost see the wheels turning in her head. "A hundred thousand? You could pay off your mortgage with that much, Jake."

"More like buy a cup of coffee with a dollar and what's in that backpack. Just how dumb does this guy think I am? At the book signing, he said it was gold ore. Remember the discourse with Cory?"

The wheels stopped turning, and she simply stared at me.

"He's lying, Bon. He also lied to me about talking to Craig, and I'm not buying his excuse for being at Appleton's. Besides, I don't have the foggiest idea who took the backpack or where to find it."

"Why do you say that, Jake?"

"Say which, that he's lying, or where to find the backpack?"

"The part about him talking to Craig Renfield, silly."

"He claims to have told Craig he would pay dearly for his copy of *Tom Sawyer* if he got it back, he supposedly said this at the signing."

Bonnie stared at me blankly.

"Two things wrong with that, Bon. First Craig left the signing before Wilson could talk to him, and secondly, Shelia's copy hadn't been stolen yet."

She thought about it for a moment then shook her head in agreement. "He must be lying about the book, too. I mean how would he know it was in the backpack?"

"A little birdie told him."

Bonnie nearly snorted, the kind of snort that would spray someone if she had been drinking anything. "You're kidding. He said that?"

"The little birdie told him Craig Renfield has the backpack, and he wanted me to go after it."

She shook her head in disbelief.

We drove in silence for another fifteen minutes before she spoke again. She was staring out her window again, looking up at Mother Cabrini's statue as I passed it. "Tomorrow's Sunday, you know."

"And after that is Monday, then Tuesday."

She ignored my smart-aleck response. "You promised you would go to church with me. So will you?"

"I'd love to, Bon, but I can't leave Fred alone so soon after being pepper sprayed."

Wilson might have lied to me, but he was in good company. I hadn't told Bonnie the whole truth. I had led her to believe I wasn't going after the backpack, for fear she would insist on going with me. Then, maybe I should have told her because now I didn't have a good excuse to skip out on the church service I had promised to attend.

"Not a problem, Jake. Bring him with you. Our pastor loves dogs as long as they are behaved and I will vouch for Freddie any day."

The service was interesting to say the least. I had been raised Catholic, so I wasn't prepared for a sermon where every other sentence started or ended in a Bible quote. I felt like a student who needed to write down all the biblical references so I'd be prepared for a pop quiz. I did, however, love the songs they sang and tried in vain to follow along.

They had a little potluck afterwards. I didn't want to stay because I hadn't brought a dish, but Bonnie insisted she'd brought enough for us both. We were in the food line when the gray-haired lady from the book store approached.

"Patty, you remember Jake, don't you?" Bonnie asked her friend.

I was holding Fred by the collar with one hand and a plate in the other. "Stay," I said, letting Fred go so I could shake Patty's outstretched hand.

"And this must be Fred," she said, reaching out to shake his paw.

The show off smiled and raised his paw.

"He sure is well behaved. Is he a Golden?"

"I think so." I wondered if now would be a good time to ask her if she'd planted the nail file. "He was a present for my daughter on her tenth birthday. I got him from a shelter when he was just a puppy, so we don't have papers to know for sure."

Patty was barely five feet tall and didn't have to bend down to pat Fred on the head. "Well, he could be the poster boy for *Golden* magazine, if you ask me. Couldn't you, boy?"

Fred didn't take his eyes off the sandwich Patty was holding in her other hand. The beggar probably thought she would give it to him if he pretended to be good.

"He's quite the watch dog, too," Bonnie said while we made our way to a nearby table. "You should have seen him chase away the burglar who broke into Jake's house." She sounded like a proud grandmother talking about her grandchild.

"And the day that woman broke into your place, Bon." As badly as I wanted to, I didn't mention it was a gray-haired woman.

"Someone broke into your house? What did they take?" Patty's surprise looked genuine enough to make me realize I might be wrong about her.

"That's the weird thing. They didn't take anything," I answered without adding the part of the burglar planting evidence to harm Bonnie.

Patty raised her left eyebrow. "A burglar who doesn't steal? That *is* strange. It reminds me of a story by Lawrence Block where his burglar planted evidence after finding a corpse in the bathroom. You didn't have any dead bodies lying around, did you, Bonnie?"

She had just taken a bite of potato salad, so I answered for her. "*The Burglar Who Traded Ted Williams.*"

Bonnie looked annoyed. "No, and I'm not a Block fan either. He's a little too graphic for my tastes."

It was my turn to eat and listen, but not before sharing my sandwich with Fred.

Patty smiled. "My all-time favorite has to be Agatha Christie's *And Then There Were None*. "She had that far-away look in her eyes, like Julie used to have when I knew her mind was somewhere else. "I think she was the first to use a fake murder. At least, the first I've ever read."

"A *fake* murder?" Bonnie asked.

"Oh, yes. It was so clever. The murderer pretended to be the first to go. Then he proceeded to kill everyone, one by one, until there were none."

Patty's phone went off just as I started to say something. "Yes, I'll be right out," she said to whoever was on the other end.

"I *do* have to get going, Bonnie," she said after disconnecting. "My ride is outside waiting." Then, turning to me she said, "It's been a pleasure meeting you again, Jake. I hope to see you and Fred next week."

"What was *that* all about?" Bonnie asked after Patty left. "You practically accused her of breaking into my home. I hope she doesn't think I put you up to it."

"Sorry, Bon, It's just that she looks so much like the woman I saw. If only we had the camcorder."

"Forget the camcorder, I know who did it." Bonnie had a grin on her face that stretched from ear to ear.

"Oh? And who could that be?"

The twinkle in her eyes made her look ten years old. "Shelia, of course. You know, and then there were none."

I didn't act surprised at her answer, for the same thought had crossed my mind. "I suppose Shelia could have faked her own murder—it wouldn't be the first time that old trick's been tried. But what is the motive? And more importantly, if the corpse isn't Shelia, who is it?"

"I haven't a clue. Maybe some tart she caught him with," she answered, staring into space. "Or maybe some homeless soul they picked up on Colfax. Yes, that makes more sense."

Bonnie was getting too excited. I had to think of a way to calm her down quickly before she had another heart attack. "Let's go over to the Little Bear, Bon. I'll buy you a drink and we can think this through."

Fred decided to add his two-cents before Bonnie could answer, and barked. Bonnie reached down to pet him. "Of course you don't want to sit out in a hot car, Freddie. What is your master thinking?"

"Okay, Bon, that was a bad idea," I said before looking at Fred and adding, "Traitor."

"That would explain the person I saw sneaking around in Renfield's kitchen," I said once we were back at Bonnie's house, and sitting out on her deck. "It could very well have been Shelia trying to hear what I had to say."

Bonnie had mellowed out after her second glass of bourbon and was no longer acting like a schoolgirl. "And I'll bet she was the one who broke into my house and planted the evidence to frame me."

I picked off a piece of meat from the chicken wing I was eating and threw it to Fred who wasn't going to leave me alone until he got his share. Bonnie had insisted on fixing us something to eat even though I was still stuffed from the church potluck. "I suppose she could have been wearing a wig, but I really don't think so. The person I saw was much shorter."

"How can you be sure, Jake? You said you didn't get a good look because she was too far away, remember?"

She had me there, memory can play tricks after a while, and now I wasn't sure what I had seen. "Okay, suppose you are right and Shelia's not dead. And suppose the corpse was a homeless person she and Craig lured into their home, but why? Why go to all this trouble to frame you?"

Bonnie took a deep drag on the cigarette she had been smoking, and let the smoke drift off before answering. "I can think of a million reasons. Like insurance, or maybe she was about to be arrested for something, or maybe it's like I said before and she came home to find her doppelganger in bed with Craig."

"Doppelganger?"

"Someone who looks exactly like her," Bonnie answered.

"I know what a doppelganger is, Bon. I was wondering what made you think the corpse looks anything like Shelia. And come to think of it, wouldn't the cops want to identify the body with fingerprints, or dental records or something? I would think that would be mandatory in a murder, case."

Bonnie squashed her cigarette in an ashtray that had once seen better days as the base of a flower pot. "There you go being a negative Nancy. I need your help to prove Shelia's alive before they arrest me for killing her. If I wanted someone to throw roadblocks in my way, I would have asked Margot."

Fred must have detected her frustration and went over to sit by her. Or maybe it was because I didn't have any more chicken wings and she did.

"Whoa, Bon. I was just playing devil's advocate. I suppose it won't hurt to check into it."

Checking into Shelia pretending to be dead consisted of a futile Internet search of police regulations on body identification. One site said autopsies were mandatory in cases of murder, while another said it was at the discretion of the family. What an autopsy had to do with identifying a body that wasn't disfigured or burnt to a crisp was beyond me, but I wasn't surprised at the search results. I wondered if I'd be better off consulting a Ouija board.

Before I wasted anymore gray-cells trying to prove something so foolish, I decided to check and see if Shelia had ever been arrested. My twisted logic told me if she had, then her fingerprints would be on file, and I could forget about giving myself the headache of going any further, because the forensic pathologist would have checked. Once more, I knew as much as when I'd started; I couldn't get that information without paying for it.

In the end, I decided my best bet would be to watch Craig's house. If Shelia were hiding there, she would have to come out sooner or later.

CHAPTER TWENTY-TWO

"That's the dumbest idea you've had yet, Jake. Just how long do you think it will be before the neighborhood watch calls the cops on you?" Bonnie said after she quit laughing. Fred and I were having our morning coffee when I told her my plan to catch Shelia. Well, I was having coffee. Fred liked his with lots of milk and nothing else, including coffee.

"I'm not going to sit out there with binoculars like some kind of pervert. In fact, I'm not even going to be there." Her look said more than any response could have. She sat there staring at me, supporting her chin with her index finger. It looked like she might slip, and cut herself with one of her rose-red fingernails from the expensive manicure Margot had paid for a few days ago.

"The Internet, Bon," I said, before she could ask. "I'll leave my car parked across the street with an IP camera on the dash that I'll disguise as a radar detector."

"You can do that? You can watch the house over the Internet?"

"You bet. And most of those cameras are twelve volts, so with the addition of a cheap adapter, it should plug right into the cigarette lighter."

She stopped supporting her chin and reached for her pack of cigarettes. My mention of the lighter must have flipped some kind of switch in her brain. "Only one problem, Einstein. You might as well write NSA on your Jeep, because it'll be about as inconspicuous as a naked hooker at communion."

The image she painted made me laugh. "And it wouldn't surprise me if Lakewood has some kind of law against parking overnight. It would be my luck they would tow it after twenty-four hours. I guess that's not such a great idea."

"No, Jake. That MP camera is a stroke of genius."

"IP, Bon, and I forgot one important fact. It needs a router to connect to the Internet. I suppose I could search for an unprotected router in the neighborhood, but that too is a crime now. But it doesn't matter. Does your nephew still have his roofing company?"

Bonnie was about to light up again, but stopped in midair with her lighter still lit. "Jonathan?" Recognition of my next move showed in her wrinkles. "Oh, no. Not that again."

It was only last year I had taken a job with Jonathan in an attempt to find evidence. Shelia had threatened me with manslaughter in the death of her husband when a barbecue grill I was using exploded in her husband's face. Long story short, I suspected

Jonathan of sabotaging the grill so I talked my way into his roofing yard to search for the faulty propane bottle.

"I need to borrow one of his pickups for a couple hours. Just long enough to install the camera on the house Cory and Jennifer were renting."

Bonnie went back to lighting her cigarette, so I continued explaining my plan. "All you have to do is call him and ask to borrow a truck to go get your treadmill. We won't need it more than a couple hours."

"Let me guess, you're going to pretend to inspect their roof. That's why you need a truck with a sign on it, so no one will ask what you're doing there."

"Close, but no banana. I'll pretend to be an estimator."

Jonathan's roofing yard was only a few miles from Cory and Jennifer's house, so even if he was tracking our mileage, I reasoned he'd never notice the little side trip we were about to make. He was waiting at the gate when we pulled up.

"I didn't think I'd see you around here after last time," he said after I parked my Jeep.

Bonnie got out, slammed her door, and spoke before I could. "Don't shoot the messenger, Jon. Jake has been good enough to help me, so I'd appreciate it if you could hold your tongue."

Jonathan smiled exactly the way Paul Wilson had that day at the bookstore when Cory had questioned him about the gold. Hannibal Lecter must have been an inspiration for both of them. "Sorry, Aunt Bonnie, but you don't need *his* help. Mom would kill me if I didn't do it for you."

Bonnie went with Jon to get her treadmill when we realized he wasn't going to let us use his truck. The ride home with Fred gave me time to rethink my plan on using the IP camera. I didn't want to run up my credit card with the purchase anyway, so in the end I decided to find another way to smoke out Shelia, if it really was her who I had seen at Craig's. For all I knew she was truly dead and the girl I saw was someone Craig had picked up at a bar. But on a whim, I decided to do a quick drive-by anyway.

Craig's new SUV wasn't in his drive, or the garage. I thought it odd he left the garage door open. If he was home, where was his car? Once again, I drove back to the Casa Bonita parking lot, put Fred on a leash and headed west on Colfax toward Saulsbury Street.

Fred stopped at a telephone pole on the corner of Pierce and Colfax. I pretended to look at some posters on the pole when I saw him lift a leg.

"This could be you, buddy, if they arrest me for what you're about to do," I said when I saw a poster for a lost dog stapled between a poster for a week old garage sale, and another for a missing woman. He didn't seem to care and went about his business anyway. I was about to scold him before I did a double take of the poster. The woman could easily pass for Shelia's sister.

I didn't know what I expected once we'd made it back to Craig's house. Bonnie's theory that they used a body double to fake Shelia's murder was beginning to make sense. Part of me was hoping his new girlfriend would answer the door and dispel my suspicions while another part didn't want anyone to answer, especially not Craig. When no one answered, I looked around at the neighbors' houses to see if anyone was watching, then casually walked down the drive toward the garage.

Most of the houses on the block had detached garages built at the back of the house. At least, those that had garages. It was an older neighborhood, built in the thirties and forties when garages were a luxury. It was obvious Craig's garage was an afterthought, built in the late fifties or early sixties, because the architectural style wasn't even close to that of the house. The garage had stucco walls and a flat roof, whereas the house was clad in asbestos siding with an asphalt shingle roof. I also discovered why the door had been left open—there wasn't one. What must have been its door, or what was left of it, was lying against a side of the garage I couldn't see from the street. It was one of those doors that consisted of two-foot panels that slid on rollers, and there was only one panel I could see.

The temptation to snoop inside was too great. "Stay here and warn me if anyone comes back, Freddie." He had been following me so closely he could have been my shadow, if I had large floppy ears and a tail.

Fred looked at me like I'd just eaten a burger and didn't give him any. "Please, Freddie. I need you to be my lookout."

He stayed when I went into the garage, but something told me it wouldn't last long so I had better be quick. I had no idea what I was looking for. If Craig had killed Shelia, would he be dumb enough to leave evidence in a garage less than twenty feet from the murder scene?

Once inside, I couldn't see anything of value. It was a small garage, with a workbench on the side that must have made it difficult to park a car larger than his old Toyota. That explained why he parked his new SUV in the driveway. A quick glance showed no tools on the bench or walls, which didn't surprise me, because they wouldn't last long in an open garage in this part of town. I was about to leave when I decided to check the floor for oil stains, but that, too, was a disappointment. The power-steering fluid I hoped to find on the floor didn't exist. The only discoloration I saw were dirty, dark, puddles of oil from a tired engine.

Fred's tail beat faster than a hammer-drill on high when I returned. "I'm happy to see you too, Freddie. Are you ready to get out of here before we get caught?,"

He barked once before heading down the driveway toward the street. I swear he acted like we had just robbed a bank. I thought for sure he wanted to get away before the posse showed up, but he surprised me. Instead of going to the car, he stopped at a trash can and barked again.

I knew him too well to ignore his outburst. "Is there something in there?"

He answered with a grin.

Once more, I looked around to see if we were being watched before lifting the lid from the trash can. "Is food all you ever think about?" I asked when I saw somebody's partially eaten, worm-infested sandwich. I was about to put the lid back and leave when I realized the worms weren't moving. In fact, they weren't worms at all. They were pieces of tape from an old cassette. But not any cassette, it was tape from a mini-DV cartridge, like the one my old camcorder used. I pushed the sandwich aside, and saw the rest of my tape. Someone had tried to destroy it by cutting it into pieces.

Fred barked before I finished gathering the larger pieces of tape into a bundle I could carry. "What now, Freddie?" He was looking toward the house.

This time the hair on the back of my neck rose. It was like one of those eerie feelings one gets when walking by a cemetery late at night. I felt someone was watching us and looked up in time to see a curtain moving inside the window facing us.

CHAPTER TWENTY-THREE

Jon waved me down after I'd turned onto Columbine Circle. His truck was parked in Bonnie's driveway with the treadmill resting on the tailgate, where he sat smoking a cigarette. I pulled in behind him instead of going up the road to my cabin.

He flipped the cigarette aside. "It's about time you showed up. I was about to give up on you."

Fred wasted no time running up to our cabin the minute I let him out. I didn't bother calling him back, for he wouldn't be much help with the treadmill anyway.

Maybe Fred didn't care if Jon burned down our mountain, but I did, and walked over to his discarded cigarette to stomp on it. "Where's Bonnie?" I asked, feeling bile rising in my stomach. I felt like telling him what an idiot he was, but held it in for Bonnie's sake.

He pulled out his cell phone from a shirt pocket, pretending not to notice me extinguishing his cigarette. "Dropped her off at the book store. She got a call from that friend of hers on the way up here.

Told me to wait for you cause you had a key." He never once took his eyes off his phone to look at me.

"Patty?" I asked, mesmerized by the way his thumbs danced on the virtual keyboard.

"I guess. She didn't say." He finally looked up from his texting. "Well Smoky the Bear, if you're ready to help me, I've really got better things to do than sit around yakking about a couple of old women."

A year ago I would have told him where he could put the treadmill, but ever since Julie died I no longer let rude people upset me. She taught me that life really is too short to get upset over ignorant people, so I bit my tongue and counted to ten instead.

I waited until Jon was gone before calling Bonnie to see if she needed a ride home.

"Thanks, Jake, you're a sweetheart, but it will be too late. I'm helping Patty inventory the store."

That didn't surprise me, for Bonnie would help anyone who asked. "Why's she doing that?"

"She came into some money and wants to buy the place. It broke her heart when she sold the store in Boulder, and now she has a chance to get back to what she loves the most."

"I'll be up awhile splicing a tape back together that Fred found at Renfield's. Call me when you're ready to come home."

"Craig Renfield's? What were you doing there?" A voice in the background told me she was using the speaker mode.

"Anyone there besides Patty?"

"No, Jake. Now tell me why you went there."

I wasn't sure who was listening, and didn't want some total stranger to think I went around scrounging through trash cans, so I blamed it on Fred. "Wilson told me that Renfield had Julie's book, so I had to see if it was true. He wasn't home, but when Fred took off chasing a cat into the backyard, I went chasing him. That's when he found the tape."

"And you think its tape from your camcorder?"

"What else could it be?"

"An old Alice Cooper tape that wore out after forty years. Craig Renfield strikes me as the type who likes decapitating chickens." I could hear Patty giggle at the remark.

"Decapitating chickens?" I asked.

Bonnie laughed. "Before your time, sonny. Alice Cooper was a rock star who used to behead live chickens on stage."

"Ask him, Bonnie," Patty asked.

"Jake, did you ever retrieve Shelia's copy of *Tom Sawyer*? Patty said it might be worth a fortune."

"Yes, Bon. You can tell her it's safe. Fred and I dug it up some time ago." I wanted to know why Patty was so interested, but I also wanted to get to work on the camcorder tape, so I didn't ask.

Bonnie said something to her friend I couldn't make out before coming back online. "Patty would like to see it when you pick me up tomorrow. Do you mind?"

"Sure. I mean, I don't mind, but I didn't tell you the best part about our trip to Renfield's. I saw a poster for a missing girl who could have been Shelia's twin. And when I was going through the trash, I swear I saw a curtain move in the house. I think you're right about the body double, and it was probably Shelia watching us. Once I get this tape back together, we should have all the proof we need to show it was Shelia who broke into your house, and planted evidence to frame you."

There was a long pause. I checked my phone to see if I had lost the signal. "Bon? Are you there?"

"Sorry, Jake. Patty was talking in my other ear. She says she knows someone who can put the tape back together, and you shouldn't try it yourself, or you may ruin it. She'll gladly pay to have it done."

Now it was my turn to pause. Obviously, they didn't think I was capable of splicing the tape back together, and maybe they were right. "Okay, Bon. We'll let the pros have a stab at it before I make a complete mess."

"Thanks, Jake. And get some rest. I'll call you in the morning to come and get us."

Patience never was my best virtue. I had no intention of waiting to see what was on the tape. I had it back together in less than an hour, but didn't have any way of viewing it without my camcorder. Then I remembered a converter I used to use so many years ago. It was a VHS cartridge that held a mini DV cassette and allowed it to be played in a VHS player. All I had to do was find the player and converter.

Somewhere around two in the morning I saw who had really tried to frame Bonnie, and knew why Patty wanted the tape so badly.

My first reaction was to run down to the bookstore, but I decided to call the cops first. It was late, and Lakewood said they would have an officer call me back when one was available, so I did the next best thing and called Deputy White. I knew it was out of his jurisdiction, but Appleton and the murdered kids weren't.

White wasn't in either, so I left a long voice mail describing Fred's find and my deduction of who had been doing all the killing.

CHAPTER TWENTY-FOUR

Bonnie was surprised to see us when Fred and I showed up at the bookstore, but Patty wasn't. The lines in her forehead, and frown on her face painted a picture of complete despair.

"You know, don't you, Jake?" Patty asked after letting us in.

Bonnie stood there with her mouth open.

"The tape, Bon. I thought it was odd that Patty didn't want me to see what was on it."

Turning to Patty, I continued. "If you had ever had children, you would know the fastest way to get them to do something is to tell them not to do it."

I finished by speaking to Bonnie. "It was Patty who planted evidence to frame you, and guess who was waiting for her in his beat-up Toyota?"

"Craig Renfield? They were in it together?" Bonnie had found her voice. "Why, Patty? I thought I was your best friend."

"No, not Renfield," I said, before Patty could speak. "He doesn't have the brains to weave such a web. I think he was hired help. The real mastermind is Paul Wilson, isn't it, Patty?"

Patty nodded her head and started to speak, but sobbed instead. I motioned toward some comfortable reading chairs and waited for the women to take a seat. She wiped her face with a tissue she must have had in her skirt pocket.

"Have you ever wanted something so bad you'd be willing to kill for it?" Patty asked.

Before anyone could answer, she turned toward Bonnie, and continued. "I'm so sorry, Bon. You know how much the store in Boulder meant to me. I thought the money Paul promised me would let me start over. I didn't mean to hurt anyone."

Bonnie's astonishment quickly turned to rage. Eyes that were larger than quarters a moment earlier were now smaller than a dime. "You set me up for Shelia's murder?" She was nearly screaming.

Fred must have sensed how upset Bonnie was, and went over to her, and put his head on her lap. She instantly calmed down. "I'm sorry, Freddie. Did I scare you?"

He answered the best he could, with sad, forlorn eyes, while keeping his tail between his legs.

She reached out to rub his ears while turning to me. "I don't understand, Jake. Why would Wilson bribe her to frame me for murder?"

"That's not why he was paying her off. Is it, Patty?" I asked.

"No." she answered without looking up.

I stood up, realizing it must have made me look like a caricature from an old black and white murder movie, but spoke anyway. "Wilson paid her to get Shelia's book, and when she wouldn't sell, Patty killed her for it."

I looked over for confirmation and took her silence for a yes. "Like she said, she was willing to kill to get back into the book business, and Shelia just happened to be in the way."

Patty finally looked up. "I didn't mean to. She was just so nasty to me, and kept calling me filthy names. She screamed for me to leave, and then picked up her nail file and threatened me. I grabbed her arm and tripped over something. The next thing I knew she was lying on the floor with the file in her neck."

I stopped pacing back and forth and looked Patty in the eyes. "Why didn't you go to the police then? It sounds like an accident to me. The worst they could have charged you with is manslaughter."

"Paul wouldn't let me. He knew the police would keep Shelia's copy of *Tom Sawyer*. He said I could forget about the book store if I didn't keep my mouth shut."

"But it wasn't the right book, so he went after my copy," I said.

Patty had regained some of her composure and didn't hesitate to answer this time. "Not him. I mean it was him, but he paid Appleton to steal it. But then Appleton decided to keep it."

"So it must have been Appleton who broke into Paul Wilson's house and stole all his notes? Is that why he killed Appleton, or did he get Cory to do it?"

"Yes and no, Jake. Yes, it was Appleton who stole Paul's notes, but it was Craig Renfield who killed Appleton. Paul found out Renfield was a drug addict and reasoned he was really stoned the night I killed Shelia, so he convinced Renfield he had killed her, and wouldn't tell if he took care of Appleton for him."

She paused long enough to chuckle at whatever she was thinking. "Paul is some kind of genius, you know. He could have been Sherlock's Moriarty. He told Renfield to borrow Cory's truck because his Toyota might draw too much attention with its bad muffler. It was really a ploy to put the suspicion on Cory if someone saw them."

"So it was Renfield driving away in the Datsun, and Wilson must have been in the F150 with Appleton?" I didn't feel like commenting on Wilson's intellectual capabilities.

"Yeah, he nearly spoiled his pants when he came back to get his notes and saw you and Bonnie standing on the deck with a shotgun."

"Was Appleton already dead then, or did they shoot him full of drugs at the park?" I knew I had to get all the details before she realized what she was saying and quit talking.

Patty's body language confirmed my fear, and she turned to Bonnie, crying again. "Please don't go to the police, Bon. I'm *so* sorry, but hanging me won't do anyone any good."

It looked like Bonnie was about to explode. "You didn't mind seeing *me* swing from a rope, and now you want me to forgive you?"

"Who do you think wrote Appleton's suicide note?" Patty answered, no longer crying. "That was my idea so the police wouldn't suspect you. I made Paul put it in the truck with Appleton."

Bonnie just stared without answering, so Patty tried pleading with me instead. "I can get your book and ring back, Jake."

"You know where the backpack is?" I asked.

"Your book wasn't in there. Not when the kids got hold of it. That was another clever lie Paul made up to get you to go after the backpack. Appleton kept all Paul's notes and his other loot in there, including Bonnie's manicure kit, which he must have found at the signing when it fell out of Bonnie's purse. He had it wrapped in a bloody shirt for some reason we will never know."

She stopped and dried eyes that were no longer wet. "Anyway, Paul thought he might be able to use your book and ring as some kind of blackmail, so he removed those from the backpack before giving it to Renfield to put in the Datsun. That idiot Renfield forgot about the backpack and left it in the Datsun.

When Cory found it, he must have realized what the notes meant, so he and his girlfriend went looking for the gold mine. That's why Paul wanted it back so badly, for his notes, not your book. He realized the notes on the table you found were copies made from the flash drive. The originals were in the backpack."

"Then where is Julie's book?" I didn't mention I thought it was Wilson who made the copies, and not Appleton, because I didn't want her to stop talking. The notes I found at Appleton's were printed on a dot-matrix printer. Appleton had an ink-jet. Only Wilson would have been old enough to own an antique printer.

Her tears were completely gone and replaced by a smile she must have borrowed from Wilson. "Are you going to the police?"

"No," I lied. "Bonnie's off the hook and if I get Julie's book, well I never heard any of this did I?"

Patty got up and walked over to the check-out counter. A minute later she came back with Julie's ring and copy of *Tom Sawyer*. She looked over at Bonnie before giving them to me. "Is it a deal, Bon?"

Bonnie nodded her head, and Patty handed everything to me.

"Thank you, Patty, but you realize you're still in trouble, don't you?"

Her eyes turned dark. "You promised!"

"Not me, Patty. You're forgetting about your partner in crime, Paul Wilson," I said, watching her eyes grow wider.

Bonnie gave me a look that mirrored Patty's.

"The tape, girls. Why else would he plant the tape in Renfield's trash and lure me into going there to find it? It's his chance to kill two birds with one tape." Any other time I'd expect a chuckle from my clever pun, but wasn't surprised no one laughed.

"But he must know I'd tell everything once that tape was discovered," Patty said.

Fred raised his head and started to growl, and we all turned in time to see Paul Wilson emerge from the back of the store.

"But you won't tell, my dear. Neither will any of you." He stood with his Hannibal Lecter smile, and an automatic pistol pointing at us.

I grabbed Fred by his collar before he did something stupid. "You're forgetting about your other partner, Paul. Renfield is bound to realize he's next on your list and confess to save his butt."

His smile grew bigger. "He won't be talking to anyone but Saint Peter. Who do you think was behind his curtains watching to make sure you took my bait?"

"That was you?"

His smile faded when he pulled back the top of his gun to arm it. "And since dead men don't tell tales, the tape should be all the cops need to think Patty killed everyone once I leave this gun in her hands."

I let Fred go so I could grab for the gun, but Fred was on him before he could get off the first round. Fred bit into his arm, and Wilson dropped the gun, but not before firing a shot through the ceiling, and then we heard the sirens.

CHAPTER TWENTY-FIVE

Deputy White tried to act like an upset parent even though he couldn't be more than a few years older than me. "I told you to leave the detective work to the professionals. Don't you realize you and your dog could have been killed?" White had come to my rescue after getting my voice mail. Jefferson County had also sent a deputy in response to my first call. They had left with Patty and Wilson once the proverbial dust had settled.

"At least he solved the case for you." Bonnie must have had enough of the deputy scolding me. "You should be giving him a medal or something."

White bent down to Fred's level and held out his hand. "What do you think, Mr. Fred? Does your owner deserve a medal? It seems to me you did more to solve the crimes than he did."

Fred barked then held out his paw for a handshake.

About the Author

Richard Houston is a retired software engineer who now lives on Lake of The Ozarks with a view to die for. He and his wife are raising their great-granddaughter, two Dachshunds, and a Golden Retriever.

If you enjoyed this book, be sure to check out the others in the series:

A View to Die For
A Book to Die For
Books to Die For
Letter to Die For

A Treasure to Die For

CPSIA information can be obtained
at www.ICGtesting.com
Printed in the USA
LVHW01s1105220418
574434LV00011B/702/P